The door swun[...] made the air wh[...] had been leani[...] knock, but the [...] unnerved her that she dropped her parcel. It landed with a dull thud at the feet of the doctor, just missing his well-polished black shoes.

Dr Eliot Cougar's dark eyebrows portrayed impatience and his black-brown eyes glared at her. 'How pleasant to meet you at last. I presume you are Nurse Gabrielle Ford?'

'Yes, sir.' She clutched her parcel tight to her stomach and held out her hand.

His handshake was firm and no-nonsense as he introduced himself.

Before he spoke again he re-read what she presumed were her references. Dressed all in black, he could have been about to attend a funeral. As long as it isn't mine, Gabrielle hastily reminded herself, and sat up as tall as she could.

He looked up suddenly, making her heart lurch. As he stroked his chin he said, 'Funny how you can get one impression of a candidate from letters and then a completely different one when that candidate arrives.'

Sara Burton was convent educated and trained as a physiotherapist at a school in the Midlands. She has worked in England, Scandinavia and North America and received her B.Sc. in Physical Therapy from a Western Canadian university. Currently she is engaged in independent research related to partial dislocations of joints in the lower limb. She is a bird fancier with special interest in homing pigeons.

Previous Titles

EXPERT TREATMENT
DR ROSKILDE'S RETURN
A MEDICAL OPINION

HEART SEARCHING

BY

SARA BURTON

MILLS & BOON LIMITED
ETON HOUSE   18–24 PARADISE ROAD
RICHMOND   SURREY   TW9 1SR

First published in Great Britain 1991
by Mills & Boon Limited

© Sara Burton 1991

Australian copyright 1991
Philippine copyright 1991
This edition 1991

ISBN 0 263 77216 0

Set in 11½ on 13 pt Linotron Times
03-9104-38756
Typeset in Great Britain by Centracet, Cambridge
Made and printed in Great Britain

CHAPTER ONE

GABRIELLE'S heart was beating a little fast as she drove up the highway towards the Northern University. Ever since she had come to this western part of Canada ten years ago the term 'highway' had intrigued her. It conjured up images of caped highwaymen with flintlock pistols and other masked robbers.

But surely on this simple journey she wouldn't meet anyone remotely like a highwayman, and if she did she had nothing of value he could steal.

Briefly, she glanced over her shoulder to check the contents of her old hatchback car. Boxes of books, clothes and odd items were piled almost to the ceiling, and then there was Jeremy's bike wedged in somehow. Not very much to show for her family's years of work in the New World. There should have been more, much more.

Her father had taken up a professor's post at a university down south. He had taught mathematics. An exacting and logical lifetime of study on that subject should have made him reasonable in his attitude to money, but he had fallen for the big gamble of the stock-market and lost every penny, even their home, when his stock had plummeted. The shock had literally killed him. And that had left Gabrielle alone with her brother Jeremy.

That was all in the past. Now Gabrielle had a new flat and a new job. She was to be a charge nurse on a women's surgical ward and Jeremy was about to start university as a pre-med student.

Itching to reach her destination, she increased speed and soon caught up with a heavy articulated lorry which was trundling in the slow lane. It was huge, a real monster, with sharp chrome edges that glittered in the sunlight.

Eager to regain sight of the clear horizon, Gabrielle hit the accelerator and pulled out to overtake.

As if the lorry was of the same mind it pulled out too, cutting almost across her path. Its giant wheels whirred blurringly close and loomed down on her. The noise of its engine was deafening. Instantly she checked her mirror and tried to shoot into the fast lane, but in her tiny car she must have been in the lorry driver's blind spot, because he continued to move across her path.

Gabrielle pulled hard down on her steering-wheel—too hard.

The car overshot to her left and careered down the high sides of the trough-shaped central reservation. A signpost appeared to approach her at an alarming speed and she frantically struggled to miss it.

Her over-correction made the car soar up the sides of the bank. She lost control, and the car turned in its flight and rolled over twice, only to settle in the bottom of the reservation.

When Gabrielle came back to consciousness she didn't know how long she had been out. Warm blood trickled from a cut on her temple and when she took in a breath she inhaled a white silky powder that seemed to cover everything and made her cough. The cough filled her with fear because it caused a sharp pain low down in her back. For a moment she dared not move a muscle.

She must have knocked her head at the back, because her vision was blurred, or was it just this white stuff that lay all around? Moistening her lips with her tongue, she recognised the taste of self-raising flour. It must have come from a half-empty bag which she had hurriedly packed into an open box—trying to save money, she thought ruefully.

Her next thought was that she must get out

of the car. But she couldn't budge. She felt helpless and trapped. Frustration built up in her chest, only to be dispelled as great tears rolled down her cheeks.

It seemed like an eternity before she heard the sound of a car door, then footsteps running towards her, and then she heard the voice.

'I'm a doctor. Let me take a look at you.'

And immediately a soothing reassurance filled Gabrielle as gentle, expert hands examined her eyes, ears and mouth. She knew he was looking for signs of internal bleeding.

'Any sharp pain, my dear?' the deep voice enquired.

'Just in my back. Nowhere else.'

'Can you move your toes and fingers? Try a few small movements.'

'Yes, that's no problem.' She felt relieved. At least she wasn't going to be a paraplegic.

All the while she felt his hands examining her arms and chest. He was so relaxed and calm, so thoroughly in control, that she imagined he was used to emergencies. Perhaps he worked in casualty.

'Did you lose consciousness at all, my dear?'

'Only for a very short while, I think.' She wasn't sure.

'Well, apart from your back and a nasty bump on your head I don't think there's anything else to worry about. I'll give you a shot for your pain.'

He must have had his black bag to hand, because within moments she felt a slight prick in her arm as the needle was inserted.

'Thank you,' she murmured. 'That feels better already.'

'You should really thank my daughter,' the doctor continued soothingly. 'My Mercedes wouldn't start this morning and she reminded me about my bag when I changed cars.'

So he was married, this competent man with the gentle voice. She didn't know why she felt a sudden disappointment.

The bang of a car door and thumping footsteps, every one of which Gabrielle could feel, heralded the arrival of a young man with a high-pitched voice. 'D'you need any help down here?' he called.

'You look like just the man we need,' the doctor answered with obvious relief. 'Stay with the young lady while I ring for an ambulance on my car phone. And I've got some shelves that slot together in my boot; I'll use them as a stretcher.'

'Don't worry, ma'am—people don't call me "John Pumping Iron" for nothing. We'll soon get you free.'

She could only glimpse John's fuzzy features

through the shattered window, but she was glad there would be two people to lift her out. 'So you lift weights, do you, John? I bet you never thought you'd be using your muscles for this,' she said faintly.

He gave an uneasy laugh. Then she asked, 'Is the doctor strong like you?'

'Oh, he's a doc, is he?' There was a moment's silence as John turned to look. 'Yeah, he's well built all right.'

As the doctor arrived back Gabrielle heard John whisper, 'Better get her out fast—I can smell petrol leaking, and the grass and every-thing out here is tinder-dry. One spark and we could all be flying up in the clouds!'

Gabrielle was aware that the doctor had somehow silently cautioned John, for he broke off talking abruptly. She could hear the sound of broken glass crunching under his feet, and if it hadn't been for the doctor's presence she thought she would panic.

The two men talked tactics briefly, then the doctor poked his head through the car window. 'We've decided to wrench open the left front door, then we'll be able to free you. If you hadn't got so much pain in your back I might have risked lifting you over the back seat and out through the rear door, but that's too risky.'

'Whatever you say,' she murmured. She

could just make out that he was dark-haired and, if his voice was anything to go by, very handsome as well.

Her rescue was smooth and efficient. John wrenched open the car and forced back the steering-wheel. But all the time the doctor counterbalanced the force by skilful use of his body weight.

Then she was transferred to the makeshift stretcher of shelves and strapped safely by the two men's belts. The doctor had been fastidious that no rotation should occur to Gabrielle's spine—this was to safeguard against injury to the spinal cord.

She was carried several hundred yards away from the wreck and lowered gently.

'Move the cars now, John; my keys are still in the ignition.' The young man didn't have to be told twice.

A large frame lowered itself on to the grass by Gabrielle, and she felt the doctor examining her facial cut again.

'What a fright I must look!' She narrowed her eyes to try to focus on him. 'The flour is everywhere, and I must have rubbed my face many times. . .'

His reply was easy. 'You'll look just as pretty as ever when you recover. This flour has actually helped you—it's acted to stop the flow of blood.'

She couldn't understand, and continued to stare blankly up at him.

'In the old days, when the Western provinces were beginning to be discovered by white settlers, they could carry very little in the way of medicines in their chuck-wagons. Flour was used to stop haemorrhaging. Without knowing, you've used an old remedy,' he explained.

She could feel his fingertips making a more detailed examination of her wound and then her scalp. His touch was tender enough, but another bruise was hidden under her long fair curls and she cried out in spite of herself.

'How stupid of me!' He was being harsh with himself. 'My ring must have frightened you. Here, I'll turn it round. Now it only looks like a plain wedding band. Don't be upset.'

'It wasn't your ring. You just brushed up against another bruise. Anyway, what is your ring? I can't see it; everything's a blur.'

'You didn't tell me about your eyes before.' He was bending close again, and she was aware of his musky aftershave.

'Didn't I. . .?' She felt confused. 'There was so much going on, I thought I did.'

'A touch of concussion. Not too bad, I think.'

He sat up again and placed her small hand in between his two large warm ones.

'What's so special about your ring, then?'

'It's a skull and crossbones.'

'Do you wear that because you're a doctor and work with bones?'

'That's one of the reasons. It was a gift. My daughter has a macabre sense of humour. She thought it was just what I wanted. I never thought it would intimidate patients.'

'Oh, it didn't. Well, it wouldn't have.'

'I'm glad you say that,' he replied slowly. 'Apparently she had the devil of a job finding a skull and crossbones for me, so I wouldn't like to disappoint her by not wearing it. Teenagers can be very sensitive, you know.'

Gabrielle knew all right. After all, she had been both sister and mother to Jeremy when he was growing up. Her mother had left the family for a man with what she called 'real money'.

Her thoughts were broken as John screeched the second car to a halt and ran out shouting, 'Hit the ground! It's burning—she's going up!'

Gabrielle was panic-stricken, then all at once a huge frame was on top of her. 'Brace yourself for an explosion. I'll lie on top of you and take the weight on my arms.'

Her eyes grew wide and white. She could

hear a crackling sound, faint but definitely disastrous. Then a mighty bang, an intense light and the sound of debris being hurled through the air and crashing to earth all around them.

Desperately she clung to the neck of the doctor on top of her. It was an instinctive self-protective gesture. She wanted to hide beneath his guarding frame. His close-shaven cheek came down hard against hers. She knew his whole body was straddling hers, but he kept his weight off her.

Trembling with fear, she clung tighter, until the rain of tangled metal and dust settled. She could not stop shaking, and strangely she thought she detected a fine tremor in the doctor's cheek now pressed so closely to hers.

Had he been frightened too? He had certainly shown no other signs. After what seemed like an agonisingly long time the fall-out from the explosion stopped and the doctor sat up.

'Are you all right, my dear?'

'Oh yes,' she replied shakily.

'God, I'm still quivering like a jelly!' John pushed his hands through his hair. 'I just threw myself on the ground and rolled up into a ball like a baby!'

'Reflex reaction of the whole body,' the doctor explained.

Gabrielle was aware that he was looking into

her eyes again—checking to see if further shock had set in. She felt calm and safe in his presence. He hadn't curled up on the ground, he had used his body to shield her and protect her spine. His heroic actions, so full of selfless concern, awed her.

She could hardly begin to thank him when the sound of the siren from the approaching ambulance rang in her ears. She fainted.

When Gabrielle returned to consciousness she was in an ambulance. A voice she did not know said, 'Don't be afraid. You've had an accident. But we'll be coming into the Bonnyville Hospital in a couple of minutes.'

'But I don't want to go to the Bonnyville. I'd rather go to the John Hind.'

'Well, that's a fine thing, giving your orders like that, young lady! We've radioed ahead. They're expecting you.'

'But all my friends are at the John Hind. I'm a nurse there. . .or I used to be.' Her voice faded.

'Is that a fact? Then we'll organise that for you.'

She could hear the man talking to the driver, explaining in a low voice. In a few minutes he returned and said, 'Gabrielle Ford—you used to be on a women's surgical ward?'

'Yes.'

'You'll be with your friends shortly, love.'
Then in a softly sad tone he added, 'They'll be
sorry to have you back and entering through the
emergency door.'

Gabrielle's mind began to work. 'My medical
insurance card and number. . .they were in the
car, I haven't got them.'

'Sure you have. Doctor at the scene gave your
handbag to me before he dashed off.'

'I don't remember him getting it out of the
car.' She spoke slowly as she tried to think.

'Oh, that doctor had everything in order
when we arrived. And very particular about you
he was. Supervised your transfer on to our
stretcher and gave details of the drugs he'd
given you. Lucky thing you had that Good
Samaritan doctor.'

'I know,' she said with conviction. 'Who was
he? I never did ask his name.'

'Don't know, miss. He said he was going to a
conference. That's why he zoomed off quickly.
He wasn't from around these parts. I'd never
seen him before.'

For the time being Gabrielle had to be con-
tent with what she'd been told. There would be
time later to find out about him and say 'thank
you'.

'You're a very lucky, girl Gabrielle.' Old Dr
Royle was peering at her final check X-rays as

she lay on her bed in one of the single rooms reserved for the treatment of staff. 'Yes, that compression fracture of your first lumbar vertebra has healed well.'

'And when can I go back to work?' Her voice was nervous.

'Good gracious, young woman, can't you just lie back and enjoy the rest?'

'No!' she almost wailed. 'I should have started my new job as charge nurse weeks ago. If I don't let them know for sure soon, they'll give the job to someone else.'

Dr Royle sighed and sat on the bed. 'Gabrielle, active nursing is out of the question for many months. Your back is still too vulnerable to work on the wards.'

She turned her head away so that he shouldn't see the tears that had started to well up. She had to earn the money for Jeremy's education.

Dr Royle spoke kindly. 'Ward work is out, but how about a stint in general practice?'

She hadn't thought of this, and so when she looked back at him her eyes were hopeful.

Dr Royle continued, 'I've an old colleague up near the Northern University. Yes, the same university that your brother will attend. On September the twelfth he has a vacancy.'

'That's the day university starts!' she cried.

'I can see the idea pleases you,' he grinned.

'I'll give Dr Cougar a ring. He's an excellent doctor, but he can be difficult at times. He wants a nurse with a very professional outlook, not a frivolous young woman. Hmm. . .yes, I think you'll fit in there nicely.'

Gabrielle was thrilled.

'Eliot Cougar trusts my judgement,' Dr Royle added. 'I won't go into the details of your accident. All he'll need to know is that I've passed you as fit to work for him.'

Towards the end of the morning Dr Royle came back with the good news. 'You've got an interview on the seventh, Gabrielle.'

'That's wonderful!' she enthused. 'I won't let you down. But tell me, what's Dr Cougar like?'

'A remarkable fellow. His life is a study of devotion to his patients. Not only has he a rich store of knowledge, but he's got a real insight into people, especially students. Many students prefer a GP rather than Student Health. He has the wisdom of a much older man.'

The image of a man just a few years off retirement flashed into Gabrielle's mind. He was probably just like Dr Royle.

She was thinking of all the possibilities that had opened up when Dr Royle said, 'Please listen, Gabrielle. . . You'll be near the university campus and you'll have a great many opportunities to meet young people like yourself.'

He leaned forward in his chair. 'And when you're lovemaking, my dear, don't go in for all that acrobatic stuff to start with. Take things gently and pick a considerate young man. Before you're discharged I'll bring you a small book on safe positions. It's something I give to all my back patients before I discharge them.'

Gabrielle went quite puce.

'Haven't you got a boyfriend at the moment?'

'There really hasn't been time. . .what with work and looking after my brother.' She lowered her eyelashes and refused to meet his frank gaze.

Dr Royle sensed her embarrassment and returned to the safer subject of her new job.

'Now, I think you'll have a very pleasant time working in that family practice. Dr Cougar has a lot of postgraduate students on his list. And when you think of the size of the campus, those students have to be fit to walk from one class to another.'

Gabrielle's colour began to return to normal.

'Poof!' exclaimed Dr Royle. 'Those students are so healthy that you'll have nothing more to treat with them than tension headaches before exams, writer's cramp and the odd physical education student who's torn a muscle.'

'I can't imagine it's going to be the holiday

camp atmosphere you describe.' Her eyes widened in astonishment.

Dr Royle's eyes twinkled. 'It's going to be just the ticket for you—wait and see.'

She thanked the old doctor for all he had done, and as they shook hands she said, 'Have you been able to find out anything about my Good Samaritan doctor?'

'Gabrielle!' He sighed. 'No, I'm sorry. And believe me, I've tried. After all, you've asked me and everyone here in the hospital every day since your admission.' He shook his head. 'No one knows of a doctor who wears a skull-and-crossbones ring.'

She said thank you again, but when she was alone she sank back on her pillows. Moments before her crash she had been thinking of bygone highwaymen and dismissing the fact that anyone could waylay and rob her on a modern road.

She had been wrong. The dark doctor had come to her aid, and stolen something of the greatest worth. He had captured her heart. And now, you never knew your luck, working near the campus and the university hospital, she might bump into her doctor with the skull-and-crossbones ring. Her pirate of the highway.

*   *   *

Gabrielle felt nervous as she cleaned a working surface in the kitchen of her new flat. She hadn't seen her brother for months, and that had been before her accident.

Jeremy had taken a summer job on the look-out for forest fires way up north in the Canadian wilderness. It was the sort of job many men cracked up under. The weeks of solitude combined with the perils of wild animals were too much for many, even though the money was good.

But Jeremy, at only eighteen, had stuck it out. Gabrielle was intensely proud of him, and for that reason and because they needed the money she had made light of her injuries, and insisted that it wasn't necessary for him to break his contract and come back to see her.

A rap on the flat door made her jump. Flinging the door wide open, she saw her brother. He was taller and more muscled than when she had last seen him. His fair hair, less curly than hers, was almost shoulder-length, and his eyes seemed bluer against the dark tan of his face.

'I'm sorry, ma'am. . .' he began. 'I must have the wrong flat.'

'Has the wilderness turned your brain, you great noodle?'

'My God! It really *is* you, Gabrielle! You

look so different.' He wrinkled his nose. 'And you've had all your beautiful long hair chopped off. . . Let me look at you. You've lost weight.' He hugged her tight. 'Are you really fully recovered?'

'I will be as long as you keep your bear-hugs on the gentle side.' She laughed; it was so good to have him back.

They sat up well into the night swapping stories. As she looked at him Gabrielle felt some small thing had broken. He was no longer her dependant, a small child to be cared for; that was something of the past.

'And tomorrow I'm going over to the drug store to get a paper,' he announced.

'Whatever for?'

'I've got a couple of days free before I register in person at the university, and I'm going to get a job.'

'That's ridiculous, Jeremy!'

'Are you absolutely certain you'll get this job with Cougar?'

'Yes. . .no. . .well, Dr Royle said the interview was only a formality.'

'In the wilderness the first thing you learn is to take nothing for granted.'

'But we're in the city!'

Against all Gabrielle's protests, Jeremy got a job on a building site. And because he was busy working he asked her to buy some textbooks from the university bookstore.

She thought she had left plenty of time to buy the books before her all-important interview, but to her horror she found her watch had stopped, and to make matters worse she was in a queue which only took cheques. She had nothing but cash on her.

She was seized with panic at the idea of being late, and without thinking rushed to the head of the cash queue and started to plead with the young man whose turn it was to be served to let her through.

'Keep your hair on, lady!' The fellow pulled her in. 'I'll get flayed alive for letting you jump the queue. Just don't turn on the waterworks.'

She thanked him profusely, and when she had paid for the books she was off and running, cursing her high-heeled court shoes and clutching desperately at the thick green-and-white-striped paper bag.

Breathless and with hair definitely dishevelled, she arrived at the practice. At the enquiry desk she blurted out her name. The receptionist, rather chubby and decked out like a Christmas tree in jewellery, looked aghast.

'Dr Cougar's been out several times looking for you, love. Quick! Straight down the corridor and last room on the left.'

CHAPTER TWO

GABRIELLE rushed along frantically until she was just in front of the last door. It was slightly ajar.

She was about to burst straight in with an abject apology when she heard a man's deep voice.

'I'm sorry, darling—it looks as though I'll be late home tonight.'

There was silence. He was talking on the telephone, no doubt to his wife. And he had sounded tired and fed up. He was speaking again in a low soft tone. 'Yes, I love you too.'

This was very awkward. Gabrielle backed away a couple of paces. She didn't want him to see her hovering at the doorway. She listened intently for the receiver to click back into place. Uncertain as to whether a sound had been just that, she stepped forward to the door.

The door swung open with such force that it made the air whoosh in front of her. Gabrielle had been leaning forward and was about to knock, but the sudden situation so unnerved her that she dropped her parcel. It landed with a dull thud at the feet of the doctor, just missing his well-polished black shoes.

He stood immobile, towering above her as she sprang back like a frightened kitten.

'I'm so sorry, sir,' she began, and hastily retrieved her parcel.

His dark eyebrows portrayed impatience and his black-brown eyes glared at her. 'How pleasant to meet you at last. I presume you are Nurse Gabrielle Ford?'

'Yes, sir.' She clutched her parcel tight to her stomach and held out her hand.

His handshake was firm and no-nonsense as he introduced himself. She had the feeling that he was only just in control of his anger. Here was a force to be reckoned with. All her confidence wilted as he spoke too softly and installed her in a well-padded chair directly in front of his black mahogany desk.

Before he spoke again he re-read what she presumed were her references. During the silence she was intensely aware of the sound of her own breathing. She tried to take deeper, slower breaths to calm herself.

His hair was thick and black and flecked at his temples with grey. And although his features were more rugged than classical he was a severely formidable interviewer.

Dressed all in black, he could have been

about to attend a funeral. As long as it isn't mine, Gabrielle hastily reminded herself, and sat up as tall as she could.

He looked up suddenly, making her heart lurch. As he stroked his chin he said, 'Funny how you can get one impression of a candidate from letters and then a completely different one when that candidate arrives.'

Stunned into two seconds' silence by his remark, she missed the opportunity to explain why she was late.

Pointedly eyeing her parcel, he said, 'Were you thinking of continuing your education here at our university? Perhaps a few night classes in preparation for your Masters in Nursing?'

'No, sir.'

'Then put your shopping on the floor, Nurse Ford. Now that you've finally arrived I'd rather like to have a look at you, and your parcel is so big that I might be mistaken into thinking you're trying to hide behind it.'

Gabrielle knew only too well that it was bad interview technique to have items cluttered on your lap. Obediently she placed the books on the floor and sat up. She was furious with herself for blushing.

Immediately she met his dark penetrating eyes he asked, 'And if you're taken on here in the general practice, what type of patients do you imagine you'll be helping to treat?'

'General patients. . .' she blurted out.

'An obvious assumption.'

'And students from the nearby university. . .'

He nodded his head slowly and forced a smile. He had not only totally intimidated her, he had made her feel very silly.

'What conditions do you think we treat in our students here, Miss Ford?'

He had now relegated her from the rank of nurse to mere Miss. She had to regain a little control of the situation. Already it seemed he had made up his mind. Her memory flew back to the conversation she had had with old Dr Royle.

Confidently, she replied, 'Students here will be young; generally they'll be fit. Conditions will include. . .influenza. . .umm. . .sore throats. . .' Her mind had gone blank. 'And tension headaches, writer's cramp and the occasional strain of a muscle or a ligament.'

Immediately she had said it she wasn't pleased with her answer.

'Wrong on almost every count.' He consulted his notes again. 'I see you haven't long been qualified yourself. Surely you can't have forgotten what it was like on campus when you were a student?'

'I was quite well when I was training——'

'But didn't you ever open your eyes and ears to the life that was going on around you? Perhaps you spent most of your time with the interns?'

She was outraged that he had intimated that her time at university had been solely a period of socialising with the medics. 'No! I concentrated on my studies and my family life.'

Fierce eyebrows rose slowly. 'Admirable pastimes,' he said sarcastically.

He continued in the same tone. 'Let me enlighten you about our students here.' Then slightly more softly, 'Firstly, all students are not young. Many mature students either enrol for undergraduate courses or come back for postgraduate education. In fact, we have several retired people who are well into their sixties.

'Our patients sometimes present us with the trivial problems that you outlined. But for the life of me I can't remember the last time I treated a tension headache. The student population presents us with the whole gamut of medical problems.'

Gabrielle didn't know why she had given Dr Cougar such a shallow answer. She knew everything he was saying. If she had just thought rationally she could have come up with a good answer. But the fact was, she hadn't.

'One final question,' he said languidly. This was going to be a short interview. 'Our university patients are special. They don't represent all aspects of intelligence. Many will go on to do great things for humanity. They may be instrumental in discovering a cure for cancer. Or they may invent sophisticated bio-electric limbs for amputees, or even produce genetic engineering advances where petroleum products are easily gathered from trees.'

His eyes were unblinking and his voice almost caressing as he came to his point. 'Now. . .what *special* qualities would you imagine we should use when treating these types of patients?'

Gabrielle was suddenly on the alert and very pleased. She recognised this type of question and the cunning, seductive way it had been put over.

It was a trick. One of her most arrogant and superior surgeons had used to love to bait his interns with a similar question, and when they fell into the trap he would metaphorically wipe the floor with them.

To give herself a few moments to collect her thoughts she paraphrased the question, then replied, 'In my opinion, sir, *all* patients should be treated with equal courtesy and respect. Like anyone else, these patients will be afraid, especially of any condition that they don't fully understand.'

She took a deep breath and continued, 'To get the best results they should be reassured and the situation explained to them. If they're really academically brilliant then you can go into a little more detail. But each treatment should be tailored to the individual and his ability to cope with his problem.'

She had heard her previous surgeon give this little speech so many times that she knew it almost by heart.

Dr Cougar didn't respond at once. Instead he stared at her for what seemed like an incredibly rude length of time.

'Well, Nurse Ford. . .' he began.

Gabrielle almost leapt out of her chair in triumph. He had reinstated her to the position of nurse!

'Well, well. You've posed me something of a mixture. From your references alone and your high recommendation from Dr Royle I would have hired you unseen. But your appearance here, late and flustered, has given me a poor opinion. Your answer to the type of university patient treated here was dismal. But, on the strength of your last answer, I'm inclined to waive my judgement.' He looked at her seriously. 'I know of your recent fracture to your spine, and I wouldn't like to think of myself as a man with no compassion. Therefore, you're hired.'

She was about to enthuse all over him, but something restrained her and all she said was, 'Thank you, Dr Cougar. You won't regret it.'

Without further comment he went on, 'Can you start work tomorrow morning?'

'I thought I was to start on Monday,' she began.

'Don't tell me there's a problem already?' He looked at her wearily.

'No. Tomorrow will be fine.' Gabrielle tried to redeem herself.

'Be here at seven-fifteen sharp.'

'Yes, sir.' She was determined not to show her surprise.

'I believe in prophylactic medicine, Nurse Ford. It's always easier in the long run. And tomorrow and Friday the university will have registration in person. Student Health have been short of staff lately, so I've volunteered to help. Do you think you can manage to help me set up an influenza prevention programme?'

Gabrielle had helped out on several occasions with the flu shots at her old hospital.

'I'd enjoy that, sir,' she told him.

Looking her up and down, he nodded, and in

an uncertain tone, as if he was having second thoughts, said, 'Seven-fifteen tomorrow?'

She assured him that she would be on time.

'Why are you staring at my hands, Nurse Ford? I don't wear a wedding ring, if that's what you want to know.'

Subsconsciously she had looked at the hands of all the male doctors she came in contact with. 'I wasn't looking for that,' she cried.

The interview was terminated very quickly as Dr Cougar ushered her out of his office and saw her to the front door.

The chubby woman who had been in Reception when Gabrielle had arrived was still there. She smiled uncertainly at her and then looked at Dr Cougar, as if to judge the situation. Gabrielle smiled back, but inwardly she felt very annoyed with herself.

The whole interview had gone badly. Even if she hadn't failed outright, her new boss thought of her as tardy and someone who put shopping before a career.

And her last *faux pas* had been the worst. Why she had even bothered to look at his fingers she didn't know. . . Of course, she had been checking for her highway doctor! He was one of the nicest men in the world. Whereas Dr Cougar was one of the most arrogant men she had ever met.

That night as she lay awake Gabrielle did some serious thinking. It was vital that she should remain employed and earning. In that case, she would do well to put all previous thoughts of the cool, clinical Dr Cougar out of her head. No good would come of comparing him to her wonderful skull-and-crossbones doctor. Dr Cougar was the man in her life now, and she had better get used to the idea.

Arriving early at the practice the following morning, Gabrielle found the place unlocked and Dr Cougar already about.

'You're an eager beaver,' he called as she entered the building. 'There wasn't time last night, so I'll show you your locker now.'

He led her through the office area, which was small and compact, and into a room that was wall-to-wall files. Off this was a small sitting-room with coffee-making facilities and a row of lockers behind a partition.

'Will you be able to find your way back to my office when you've changed?' he asked with a crooked smile.

'I think I can manage.' She wouldn't let his light needling bother her. Today was a new start.

As soon as she had changed into her white

uniform and disposable cap she retraced her steps and found him.

Without preliminary he began, 'We'll be going over to the big gym in the physical education building shortly. I'll drive all the stuff over, but first let me explain a few things. It's not compulsory to have the flu jab. Any student can have it as long as they've paid their Student Health fee. So ask to see their ID cards and write down their names and numbers on this pad.' He held up a clipboard containing a thick wad of paper.

He sat on the edge of his desk and eyed her with the glint of a smile. 'There are twenty-four thousand students enrolling this year, so I want to see if you're capable on the practical side of things.

Gabrielle's face fell in horror. 'Are you telling me I've got to give injections to twenty-four thousand in two days?'

'No.' He threw back his head and laughed. 'If you had some sort of machine-gun that fired at the students as they stood in lines you might do it. But then they wouldn't get the individual touch, would they?'

She had to admit that he was remarkably handsome when he laughed and smiled like that.

'Now, Nurse Ford, let's see exactly what kind

of a nurse you are. Just treat me as a young student and give me my injection.'

She hadn't expected to demonstrate her clinical skills on him. Without wasting time she pulled the chair out from behind his desk, set it in the middle of his office, and said, 'May I have your student ID, please? Just for the paperwork.'

He withdrew a card from his breast pocket and handed it over. Of course, it wasn't a student card, it was a library one. But it would do nicely for this role-play.

'Take off your shirt and jacket and sit on the chair, please, Eliot. I won't be long.'

He did exactly what she told him, while she went through the motions of entering his particulars on the notepad.

She handed back his card and asked, 'Which is your dominant hand?'

'My what hand?' he replied, looking blank.

The man was obviously used to playing games. Behind his actor's eyes Gabrielle thought she glimpsed the hint of a smile. She'd just have to play along with him.

'Which hand do you use most of the time? Which hand do you write with?'

'My right.'

'Very well, I'll give the injection in your left arm.'

She showed him how to position his arm with his hand on his hip and his elbow at right angles to his torso. It was difficult not to be affected by his maleness. The muscles in his chest and shoulders were well developed and she doubted if he had a layer of fat on his body anywhere.

She continued in her role play. 'Now, Eliot, this will feel like a slight prick. It won't hurt.' Carefully she inserted the needle and gave the injection. As she swabbed the puncture hole afterwards she said, 'You can put your clothes back on again.'

As she disposed of the needle she was aware of dark eyes following her every move. Definitely she was under intense scrutiny.

When she turned round again she noticed he had not bothered to even put on his shirt. Still sitting there in a state of semi-undress, he made her feel embarrassed.

'Not bad.' He spoke at last, breaking the silence. 'Not bad at all, Nurse Ford. But. . .' There had to be a 'but'. 'If I'd been a young girl just entering university I wouldn't have been at all pleased to have been sitting in front of an open gym full of people with my blouse off.'

He really was taking this acting game a bit far.

'I only thought of you as a man,' Gabrielle began, startled.

'I'm glad you noticed.' His lips curved into a stealthy smile. 'But what if I hadn't been?'

'No problem. *You* can take some mobile screens over to the gym when we pack your car.'

She had sounded too officious. She hadn't meant to. But with this man she was never sure if he was sincere or if he was laying a trap. The trick question at her interview was still fresh in her mind.

Eliot Cougar did not reply, just nodded his head slowly. Then, 'You did well to ask which was my dominant hand. As you must know, the arm can be a bit sore at first, and these students will be taking reams and reams of notes once classes start. By the way, I once had a patient who didn't know what I meant when I asked which was his dominant hand.' He laughed, crinkling his eyes up. 'One more thing.'

Gabrielle thought he was about to deliver some serious instruction.

'If we're ever at a party playing charades I want you to be on my team.'

This sentence stunned her. This Dr Cougar was totally unpredictable. 'We used to play charades a lot when my family was all together,' she said with a soft reminiscence.

The look he gave her was penetrating yet gentle. But he said nothing more on the subject.

In the physical education gym, which was large enough to lay two football pitches, many students were already milling around and chatting. Dr Cougar led Gabrielle to a small area by one of the main doors.

'There are screens here!' She was shocked. There hadn't been any danger at all of a young girl being exposed.

'Of course. I was only testing during my role-play.'

Tricky, dark devil, she thought. I'd better stay on my toes with you.

CHAPTER THREE

IF GABRIELLE had thought Dr Cougar cool and calculating at her interview, and a man who enjoyed adult games with women, then she had to review her negative opinion on one point.

Eliot Cougar was an excellent doctor. Giving flu injections was a repetitive and tedious job, but he made each student feel at ease, and always managed to make the treatment individual by asking them about their courses.

It didn't surprise Gabrielle that the queue for injections grew longer and longer, as the word got about that handsome Dr Cougar was at work. And she slowly admitted to herself that she enjoyed working with him.

But she still held reservations. Had he volunteered his time for the students solely as a favour to his colleagues in Student Health? Or had he just jumped at the opportunity to meet literally hundreds of young girls—all of whom obviously became instant admirers?

On her first official day at the practice Gabrielle was introduced to the other staff and the doctors, mainly older, retired men. They gave her a warm welcome which made her feel very at home.

'Before we start work, I think you deserve your flu jab.' Dr Cougar led the way to his office, where he pulled out a chair for her. 'After all, now I've got a new nurse I don't want her coming down sick. You're right-handed, aren't you?'

'Yes. How did you know?'

'I've been watching you. Now just pull up this short sleeve of your uniform—I don't think it'll be necessary for you to undress further.'

When he touched her she felt a flutter of excitement—or was it just nervousness? To control this mounting emotion she concentrated on a painting on his office wall.

Something about his manner made her mind fly back to the time she had received the pain-killing injection at the site of her accident. For a split second her memory was hazy and she relived that time out on the highway. She must have been so caught up in that bygone past that she didn't hear Eliot Cougar speaking.

He waved his open hand in front of her eyes. 'You can come back to the land of the living now. You've had your injection.'

Turning to face him, she was momentarily disorientated. Then with an effort she pulled down the short sleeve of her uniform. 'I didn't feel it at all.'

'Just as it should be,' he laughed. 'Then I give intramuscular injections as well as you, Nurse Ford.'

That was a compliment, Gabrielle thought, and she felt irrationally pleased.

She put her quivering feelings down to the fact that the flu jab had reminded her of her dream doctor. That was it. It was just an overflow of her dreaming emotions.

After collecting up the files for the morning patients she made her way back to Eliot's office. He had a broad smile. 'What have you brought me?' he asked. He glanced through the names on the buff-coloured files.

The first patient was a middle-aged lady in a most expensive designer tweed suit. She was carefully made up, but her worried expression set her pretty features off at ugly angles.

'Back again, I see, Mrs Grey,' Eliot greeted his patient with a reassuring smile. 'Is it the same problem?'

'No, doctor, no problem with my tonsils today, thanks.'

'Then how can I help you?'

'It's the headache, Dr Cougar. It's like a tight headband.'

'Have you been in an accident, Mrs Grey? Or fallen off a chair and landed badly?'

'No, Doctor, nothing that I can remember.'

He stood back, considering his patient with sharp intensity. 'Jacket and blouse off, then, so that I can examine you properly.'

Gabrielle was about to help the patient when Eliot restrained her with a gentle hand. She knew that he wanted to watch Mrs Grey for any unguarded signs. Then he was reassuring throughout his examination, explaining to his patient why he carried out the tests.

'There's no neurological problem that I can find,' he finished.

'What does that mean?' enquired Mrs Grey as she cautiously pulled on her blouse again.

'It means that as far as I can see there are no disc problems in your neck. Now, I'd like you to go for a neck X-ray over at the university hospital. It's just a formality, but no neck should ever receive treatment without one.'

As she dressed he watched her again. 'How's the family?' he asked her.

'Fine,' she smiled. 'My husband is away again, but I can cope with that now.'

Eliot sat with one leg on the plinth. His relaxed attitude was to encourage his patient to talk.

Mrs Grey continued. 'When my husband first

started these business trips I used to get so depressed. I'd just cry and cry.'

'That wasn't clinical depression, Mrs Grey. That was the natural effect of missing someone.'

She nodded. 'I coped because I went back to university here, just part-time. But I have enjoyed myself. My daughter is at school, so it's easy to fit in, and it keeps my brain going. In fact, I've been a great help to my daughter with her homework.'

'That's the ticket!' Eliot was grinning. 'How have your marks been?'

Mrs Grey was more relaxed now; she did not hold herself so rigidly as she leaned back on her chair for this social chat. Gabrielle noticed that she lifted her head quite easily to look into Dr Cougar's eyes. Cunning of him, she thought, to position himself so that she had to move her neck.

'I got a six in my summer session—I was really proud. You know that summer classes go at a galloping pace. We crammed a whole term's work into three weeks, and our prof didn't leave anything out.'

'A six is a very presentable mark.' He nodded. 'How did your daughter take to the idea of your being away from home, and studying in the school holidays?'

Mrs Grey pulled herself up with real pride.

'Oh, she was on a working holiday herself, Doctor. A ballet course, just like the professionals would have, with anatomy lessons and visits to see top-class ballet companies.'

'Sounds like you're very organised and happy.'

'Yes, I really think we are.'

When she had gone, Eliot turned to Gabrielle. 'If her X-rays are clear, I might have to think about the possibility of tension headaches. And if that's so, I wonder what's the cause.'

Gabrielle resisted the temptation of reminding him that at her interview he had claimed never to have treated a tension headache.

Then Eliot looked at her very seriously. 'Thanks for staying with me throughout that examination, Nurse Ford. And I'd like you to remain whenever I see women.' He sighed. 'Lately, a few of my colleagues have had to put up with. . .unfortunate insinuations. . . Some young girls have insinuated that they've suffered sexual impropriety at the hands of their doctors. . .'

Gabrielle knew this to be true, and totally unfounded in the vast majority of cases.

'Don't worry, Dr Cougar,' she reassured him. 'I'll always be present to protect your professional reputation.'

He looked at her from under such serious dark eyebrows that she knew he felt vulnerable. And she chided herself for having thought of him as a man who only helped out with students because he enjoyed working with partially undressed girls.

Gabrielle's first full day at the practice had been hectic. And the continual concentrated effort to do everything efficiently in a new set-up had left her with the dull throb of a headache. Walking briskly towards the campus, she decided that she'd have to take a couple of aspirins if it didn't clear soon.

She had arranged to meet Jeremy at his carrel on the fourth floor of the Newton Library. A carrel was a little desk where a student could lock away his books, and her brother had spent some of his money on one. He would have preferred to be in the medical library, but places there were like gold dust.

As she walked between the impressive campus buildings, and pushed her way through a throng of some of the twenty-four thousand students, she understood why some people found the place intimidating. And why some students, especially those who found the pace of study tough, could crack under the pressure.

She had no worries about her brother on this

score, though, especially as he now boasted that he could cope with anything. His spell in the Canadian wilderness had given him great confidence.

'So my little brother's working away like a model student,' she whispered, leaning over his carrel.

'Gabrielle!' he cried, then checked, his hand over his mouth, and went on in an undertone, 'I've got to copy something out. I'll only be five minutes, then I'll be with you.'

Her headache was coming on strong, threatening to ruin her evening. She had a couple of aspirins in her handbag, so she told Jeremy she was going to look for a drink of water. He nodded without looking up as his pen flew over his blank exercise book.

Luckily she found a water fountain in the washrooms and a machine that dispensed paper cups. She downed the aspirins, and they stuck in her throat like two old-fashioned gobstoppers.

The headache was winning. She sipped the water. It was cold and refreshing. The tablets would act soon if only she could swallow them. While she was preoccupied with thoughts of the day, she placed her cup on the carrel behind her brother's. She did not see a small notice, handwritten and stuck on the desk with Sellotape. It read, 'This carrel is taken. Clear off!'

Suddenly she looked up into the irate face of a young student.

'Out, lady. Out of my carrel!' he hissed. 'If you can't read, you shouldn't be at university, you should be back in kindergarten!'

Gabrielle was so taken aback by this unexpected attack that she stood up jerkily and knocked the paper cup over. Luckily only a few drops remained, but all the same they trickled out on to the top of the carrel, leaving two glistening marks.

The commotion made Jeremy spin round. 'My sister doesn't want your crummy carrel. Don't be so rude!' He stood up, and Gabrielle caught a wild look in his eyes that was matched by the other student's.

'Please, boys! That'll do. Calm down, or I'll have to ask to hold your coats—and that's not necessary.' She spoke to the young man. 'I'm sorry. I was only sitting here for a moment. . .'

The student dumped his books on his carrel and made a sweeping gesture to wipe away the water stains. His eyes caught hers and he suddenly stopped. 'I might have known it'd be you. *You* nearly got me scalped in the bookstore!'

'What's he drivelling on about?' said Jeremy irritably, and stood very close to his sister.

All at once Gabrielle knew, and this was the

last young man on campus that she would have wished to upset.

'It's all right, Jeremy.' She placed a light restraining hand on her brother's arm. 'I owe him my job.'

Jeremy stopped mumbling and looked blank.

Gabrielle stood square between the two men and said, 'I was late for my interview with Dr Cougar. It was the day I bought the genetics books. Thanks to this young man, who let me jump the queue, I didn't lose the job.'

Jeremy was suitably silenced. He hadn't known any of these facts before.

She turned to the student again and introduced herself and her brother. 'I can't thank you enough. Will you let us buy you supper? And I promise never to use your carrel again.'

The student's face creased into a grin. 'You're on! As long as it's Chinese food.'

This was a stroke of luck, because Jeremy was keen on it too.

'I'm Brooker.' The young man held out his hand. 'And I'm glad we're all civilised enough to sort this out amicably. I didn't fancy going through a whole year trying to do my studies behind an enemy.' He thrust his chin at Jeremy, who fortunately had dropped all his scowling looks.

All three made their way to the Chinese

restaurant that Brooker recommended. Remarkably, Gabrielle found she had lost her headache.

Brooker talked non-stop. She had time to study him as they ate. He was very good-looking with his straight-cut fair hair and his eyes of china blue. He could have modelled for a classical painting of Narcissus. But he was thin—too thin, Gabrielle thought.

Unlike Jeremy, who dressed in any old jeans and a jumper, Brooker wore neat cords and a thick-knit patterned jumper that must have cost the earth. He was very designer-looking.

For all this perfect front, Gabrielle thought there was something that did not add up about him.

'I'm studying sociology,' he told them proudly. 'My parents were furious with me. You see, my father is a professor of physics and my mother's a professor of classics. They were mad when I chose sociology. It's neither a science nor an art subject to them.'

Gabrielle could see all too well. But Brooker looked happy enough about his choice. He was very impressed by Jeremy and his acceptance into the pre-med programme.

'You'll have to work your socks off to enter medicine,' he sighed. 'Still, if you study hard enough you should make it. It's a matter of organising your time and never getting behind with your studies. I'm organised, you see, and that's why I'm a straight nine student.'

It was Gabrielle's turn to be impressed. To be a straight nine student you were in the top three per cent of all your classes, and that was a supremely difficult feat. 'I suppose you have to show your parents that brains can be as good in any subject,' she remarked.

'That's it. That's it exactly.'

Gabrielle could feel Brooker warming towards her, and she was glad. If he studied behind Jeremy he was likely to be a good example. Not that Jeremy slouched off from his work. Still, he wasn't a straight niner, but almost.

Jeremy spoke up. 'I think our carrels are in a good place. It's very quiet up there on the fourth floor. It'll suit us if it's as quiet as a morgue all year long.'

Brooker laughed. 'That isn't the sort of phrase a successful young doctor should use!'

'Quite right.' Jeremy saw the joke. 'I'll strike it from my vocabulary immediately.'

So they passed a pleasant evening and parted as friends. Gabrielle and Jeremy started their walk home and Brooker made his way across to the library.

Their footsteps clanged and reverberated as

brother and sister marched across the high level bridge that spanned the river.

They walked on without talking for a while, then Jeremy stopped and leaned against the side of the bridge. He poked his head through the openings in the criss-cross girders. Gabrielle did the same, but not for long, as the height made her feel giddy.

'Did you know that students try and commit suicide by jumping off this bridge?' Jeremy asked.

'Jeremy, you're full of morbid thoughts! First you liken the fourth floor of the library to a morgue, and now you're on about suicide. Are you considering being a coroner?'

He laughed. 'No, I think I'll stick to treating the living.'

Gabrielle walked close to her brother's side. 'How was your first day of lectures?'

'Just great. Our professors are all pretty average, except for Dr Ann Stamp. She lectures in genetics.'

By the way Jeremy's eyes were sparkling Gabrielle knew Dr Stamp must be good-looking. 'Is she very beautiful as well?'

'Stunning.'

'My brother has a fickle heart,' she laughed. 'Looks as if you've completely forgotten that

charming young girl who adored you at high
school.'

'Who. . . Oh, yes,' he smirked. 'Seeing that
I'm in medicine, I know all abut these things.
The human heart is the strongest muscle in the
entire body.'

Gabrielle raised her eyes and giggled. Then
for some reason she thought of Dr Cougar. He
must have broken a few hearts; he was certainly
handsome enough.

Early the following morning, before patients
had arrived at the clinic, Gabrielle had just
handed Eliot the patient files. He sat at his
office desk scanning them, when an elegant
woman, dressed as if she had stepped straight
from the pages of *Vogue*, entered.

'Darling Eliot!' She installed herself between
Gabrielle and the doctor.

He leaned well back in his chair and raised
dark eyebrows approvingly. 'Claudia! How
did the conference in Las Vegas go? It looks
as if you found time to do a bit of shopping
too.'

'Some lectures were good, but oh, some
others were a frightful bore, and not at all
well researched. I could have done better
myself.'

An amused smile flickered about his mouth.

'And I'm sure you will. Now, let me introduce my new nurse. Nurse Ford, this is Dr Claudia Huntridge. She works full-time here.'

Claudia Huntridge extended a gracious hand clad in a white leather glove. After the formalities were over she stepped back and said, 'My, how pretty you are! If you're as efficient as you're pretty-looking, we shall have an asset. But then Eliot always did like to surround himself with beautiful objects.'

Immediately Gabrielle felt on her guard. Those glittering green eyes shot warnings at her. She would have to be on her mettle and make sure that Dr Huntridge could find nothing in her work to complain about.

After excusing herself, Gabrielle set about checking the medical stocks in the treatment cubicles directly opposite Eliot's office. And she couldn't help but overhear.

'Darling, I'd so love to see you tonight. It's been simply ages!'

He cut in swiftly, 'Sorry, Claudia, not tonight. And you've been away less than a week.'

'But I need you, Eliot. And I've bought in some of your favourite strawberry cheesecake. Say you'll come.' Her voice was sweet and seductive.

'I eat very well at home. You know I can't

come out as I used to. I've got family commit-
ments now.'

'Don't I know it!' Gabrielle only just heard
this exasperated cry. 'I need your help on my
latest paper for the *American Journal of
Medical Science*.'

'You finished that months ago, Claudia.'

'I know, but the editors have sent it back
demanding revisions. I'm sure it's good enough
to be published as it is. But you know what
they're like—finicky.'

'Bring it here tomorrow. We can go over it
then.'

'The deadline is tomorrow, Eliot. Please say
you'll come. With your brains it'll only take a
few minutes. You know you're wasted here.'

'Don't start all that again, Claudia.' He
sounded terse. 'Very well, I'll try and slip out
when she's asleep.'

There was a long silence. Gabrielle listened
intently. What was that clothes-horse of a
woman doctor doing to him? Suddenly she
didn't care. A rising tide of fury welled up
within her.

So you cheat on your wife, do you, Dr
Cougar? You're despicable! she thought. And
just when I was about to be impressed by your
methods with patients. . .and. . .perhaps to like
you a little.

Gabrielle had agreed to protect Eliot's professional reputation, but now she viewed his personal reputation with distaste. His late-night affair with Claudia had shot that to ribbons!

CHAPTER FOUR

'I SEE you've met the fly in the ointment.' Ruby Pearly, the receptionist, eyed Gabrielle knowingly. 'Dr High and Mighty still in with Dr Cougar, then?'

'Yes, I believe so,' Gabrielle replied softly. They were in the reception office, so there was no need to talk quietly, but Gabrielle was wary.

Ruby was sitting at her desk typing a letter.

'Come closer, Gabrielle.' She beckoned with her finger. 'Take some advice from one who knows. Keep on the right side of Dr Huntridge. You've got one of the qualities she dislikes in nurses.'

'What's that?' Gabrielle was alarmed. At all costs she mustn't lose this job.

'Like the nurse before, who said she was leaving to work nearer her boyfriend, but I didn't believe her. . .you're pretty.'

'But that's got nothing to do with anything!' Gabrielle flushed.

'I'm afraid it has, love. With looks like yours, she'll be terrified that Dr Cougar will be interested.'

'That's highly unlikely,' Gabrielle said hotly, remembering what she had just overheard.

Ruby lowered her voice and whispered, 'There's only one female in our Dr Cougar's life at the moment, and that's really put Claudia's nose out of joint. . .'

Gabrielle heard no more because Dr Huntridge herself, now dressed in a tailored white coat, glided up to her.

'Eliot's told me that he doesn't need you straight away, so I want you to assist me.'

'Certainly,' replied Gabrielle smoothly. It had been fortunate that Claudia had obviously heard none of her conversation with Ruby.

Assisting Dr Huntridge was an enlightening experience. The woman doctor was very precise in all her actions, very particular that all procedures should follow the textbook methods. Gabrielle thanked her lucky stars that everything she did was correct.

But for all the doctor's efficiency, she managed to convey a coolness towards her patients which did not help. And near the end of the morning Gabrielle was dimissed with a polite, 'That will be all, thank you, Nurse,' and left feeling like a first-year student.

As all the cubicles were tidy and her help was no longer needed, she took a turn on the reception desk. Ruby Pearly was typing up some notes that one of the elderly doctors had put on tape. She had to concentrate hard because he was not used to the machine and frequently made amendments after she had typed a sentence.

With Ruby concentrating hard on the voice in her headphones Gabrielle was virtually alone. The telephone in Reception buzzed. She turned to answer it, and as she did so she didn't see a young girl approach the desk.

Behind Gabrielle's back she leaned across the front desk and studied the appointments book. When Gabrielle had taken the message she looked around and asked, 'Can I help you?'

'I'm Cathy Morris. I've an appointment at eleven-thirty.'

Gabrielle surveyed the book. 'You're a bit early. Dr Huntridge is busy at the moment. So if you wouldn't mind waiting. . .'

The girl had a mischievous smile. There was something curious about her as she walked away and sat down to read. Her body was thin and underdeveloped. She sat with her legs crossed, hunched over her books.

Ruby called out in despair, 'Oh, this infernal dictaphone! I'll have to go and ask Dr Ansty exactly what he's trying to say.' And off she went.

A few moments later Eliot wandered into the

reception office. Before he could say anything the young girl caught his eye and he called out, 'Trish! Why are you sitting there? Are you playing at being a patient? Why didn't you come straight in to see me?'

'I'm waiting for my eleven-thirty appointment, just as the nurse told me.'

This innocent-sounding statement caused Eliot to look daggers at Gabrielle. He turned to the girl again. 'Trish, go into my office and wait for me there.'

When she was out of earshot Eliot turned back to Gabrielle. He was obviously furious about something, and she was the cause.

'When my daughter comes in here I expect her to be shown straight in to see me. Don't keep her hanging around here, Nurse!'

'But——'

'No buts. Just remember in future.' He strode off before Gabrielle could explain the situation, and she was left to fume.

She hardly had time to take another two telephone appointments when Eliot came back with his daughter. Gabrielle was infuriated by his haughty manner as he addressed her. 'I'm going to drive my daughter over to the dentist. It's not far away, so I should be back before my next patient.'

As father and daughter went out through the

front door, the girl looked over her shoulder and winked broadly.

Cheeky little monkey! thought Gabrielle. I'm in a nice pile of trouble, thanks to you.

To keep her temper under control she busied herself tidying the many scattered magazines that lay on the tables in the waiting area. She had scarcely finished when she saw Eliot and his young charge striding back. He was marching Trish in, with a very authoritative arm about her shoulder. The girl was looking down at the floor and cast a wary eye at Gabrielle.

'In my office, Nurse Ford,' ordered Eliot in a gruff tone. He looked furious.

Not wanting a scene in Reception, Gabrielle led the way silently.

'Nurse Ford, sit down, please.' He indicated a chair in his office. 'My daughter has something to say. Speak up, Trish.'

The cheeky smile that Gabrielle had seen when the girl first entered Reception had been completely wiped off her face. She was trembling slightly and her voice was a mere whisper. 'I'm sorry I got you into trouble, Nurse Ford.'

There was an awkward pause.

'Go on, Trish,' her father urged.

'I promise it won't happen again.' Her voice died away and she seemed to shrink into her body. In fact she looked so pathetic, especially standing next to the looming figure of Eliot, that Gabrielle couldn't be cross.

'I accept your apology, Trish. After all, no harm was done.'

Her father spoke. 'Lucky for you Nurse Ford has such a forgiving philosophy.'

Trish stood silent again, holding her books close to her buds of breasts.

'All right.' Eliot spoke roughly. 'Say goodbye to Nurse Ford. Wait for me in the car—I'll be a few minutes.'

The girl said an almost inaudible 'goodbye' and left with her head bowed.

'Please forgive my daughter, Gabrielle,' Eliot began a few seconds after the door had closed silently. 'You see, I adopted her. She's my late brother's child. Sadly my brother and his wife died abroad. . .' He hesitated. 'Trish calls me Daddy because that's what she wants. . . And now I'm finding out that things don't always go smoothly in a one-parent family.'

A lot of things suddenly made sense. So Eliot did not cheat on his wife. He was going to leave his *daughter* to help Claudia with her latest publication. Gabrielle felt relieved. The fact that she had been set up as some kind of joke by Trish and then bawled out by Eliot seemed inconsequential now. 'I see,' was all she replied to his worried look.

'I'm sure you can't understand everything, however well-meaning you are, Gabrielle. There's been no time in your short life for babies, and I don't think *you* are a single parent. It's not at all easy, you know. . .although I thought at first that I could manage with no trouble.'

'You're wrong, Dr Cougar. Well, I haven't exactly been a single parent, but when it was just my father and my brother I did all Mum's work, and now it's only my brother and I. . . Well, I feel as though I should be like both parents to him at times.'

Eliot listened with his eyes wide open. 'I didn't know any of all this, Gabrielle.'

'It's not a problem; we manage very well.'

'I'm sure you do. How old is your brother?'

'Nearly nineteen.' She laughed. 'Not so little really.'

'Ah, but a young man isn't such a problem as a teenage girl, is he?'

'I think you're right.'

'Listen, Gabrielle, I have to go now. But if I feel I need to talk to someone about Trish, would you give me a few minutes of your time?'

Gabrielle was flattered. 'I'd be delighted to help. . .any time.'

The door swung open softly and Claudia

Huntridge stood framed in the archway. Pretending to look startled, she said, 'Oh, excuse me, Eliot—I thought you were in here alone. Could you spare a few moments. . .?'

He was halfway to the door before he spoke, 'I'm in a rush now, Claudia. Trish has to go to the dentist.'

'Of course, darling. You go. I'll see you later.' As soon as he was out of earshot she turned to Gabrielle. 'No, don't get up, Nurse. I want a few words with you.'

Gabrielle sensed danger. Claudia installed herself gracefully on Eliot's desk chair and made herself comfortable. The proprietorial way she leaned back in his chair irritated Gabrielle. Claudia was making her position very clear already.

She began, 'I couldn't help but overhear, Nurse Ford. When you were telling Eliot of your one-parent position I wasn't surprised. I had you down as the sort of girl who gets pregnant by a doctor because she either wants him to marry her or because she wants in intelligent baby——'

'As you were listening you'll know full well my position isn't anything like that.' Gabrielle's voice was cold.

'No, my dear. And I'm telling you this. It's perfectly all right by me that you go on playing the good little mother role to your brother. But don't get any ideas about Dr Cougar.'

'Dr Cougar?' Gabrielle couldn't understand.

'I can see you trying to inveigle yourself into his life. Playing up to him by saying you'll give him advice about Trish.'

'That was his idea, not mine.'

'Listen carefully, Nurse Ford.' Claudia leaned across the desk, her eyes glittering. 'Eliot's taken. We're engaged—unofficially, of course.'

Gabrielle didn't believe her.

Claudia went on, 'It's Trish, you see. We both decided to give her a little time before we got married—to help her settle in better, you understand. We've already been on holiday as a family.'

It sounded logical to Gabrielle. But Claudia was hardly stepmother material.

'Keep this information to yourself, Nurse Ford. For the sake of the child, you understand.'

Gabrielle nodded.

'And for heaven's sake don't repeat any of this to that old gossip Mrs Pearly. She's always giving the child sweets and things whenever she's here, and she flutters around her like an old hen.'

Ruby Pearly might chatter on a bit, but Gabrielle knew she was a kindly soul.

'Have you got a boyfriend of your own, Nurse Ford?'

'I don't see that that's any of your business,' Gabrielle said coldly.

'As long as you don't encroach on my affairs.' The woman doctor's voice was hard and cutting. 'If you took a bit of trouble about your appearance, added a touch of make-up here and there, you'd look quite tolerable. Of course, that wouldn't be at all appropriate for your work here.'

Gabrielle had got the message loud and clear. It was 'hands off Eliot!'

They parted politely, but the cold mutual hostility remained. To Gabrielle it was the threat to her job that troubled her most.

The following morning just before lunch break Claudia walked up to Gabrielle. She was all smiles outwardly. 'Nurse Ford, would you be so kind as to do me a favour?'

'Of course.' They were being formal and polite to each other.

'Good—I knew I could rely on you. Eliot and I are lunching out, so I simply haven't the time. Be a dear and get photocopies of these medical articles. You'll find the journals in the William Harvey Library on campus. It won't take you a minute; the campus is just a few steps away.'

Gabrielle studied the information that Claudia had written on a piece of paper. 'This should be easy enough. Yes, I'll have it done before you come back.'

'So kind of you! I've got the exact money for the machine in this envelope.'

'How thoughtful.' Gabrielle couldn't help thinking that this little exercise was designed to keep her away from Eliot.

In front of the main entrance to the William Harvey some builders had left their materials. A pile of sand and cement, a shovel and some bricks were scattered about carelessly.

Rounding a corner, Gabrielle came face to face with a big black dog. It was lying half asleep in the pale sun. This was not the sort of dog to pick an argument with. It was a Doberman pinscher and big for its breed.

Sleepy black eyes blinked up at her as she carefully edged her way past and made towards the steps. To her discomfort it lifted its head, yawned lazily and showed a sparkling set of brilliant white teeth.

'Good dog,' Gabrielle said in a wobbly voice.

She needn't have feared. The black-brown beast dropped his head on his paws and closed his eyes. No one is of any interest to you except your master, she thought. Jeremy had spoken about a big Doberman. He had seen it sitting outside the university buildings and jumping for joy after classes when its master collected it.

Once inside the library Gabrielle dismissed all thoughts of the dog. Claudia might pose more of a vicious threat than that dog if she didn't carry out this errand to her satisfaction. And she didn't want to give her any ammunition for dismissal.

She soon found her way into the medical section. It wasn't easy to find all the journals Claudia had requested, but with the help of a librarian she located a Japanese publication.

How odd, thought Gabrielle as she stood in the enclosed room where the photocopying machine was housed. This article that Claudia wants is all in Japanese calligraphy. It's not written in an English translation. She shrugged. Perhaps Claudia read Japanese fluently. Perhaps she had a friend who could translate. Anyway, that was what she had asked for and that was what she'd get.

The job hadn't taken very long. There was still time for Gabrielle to have a snack on campus, and if she could find Jeremy sitting at his carrel then they could go together. She walked out of the building with a light heart.

Loose gravelly substances lay scattered on the steps, but as Gabrielle was deep in thought she did not notice. Her foot slipped on the steps and she lurched forward, thrown completely off balance.

The black Doberman at the bottom looked up suddenly, now alert. To stop herself falling on the dog, Gabrielle threw her weight to the left and her arms in the air. The photocopies that she had so carefully collected went up also and floated down on top of the Doberman's head.

Luckily Gabrielle landed safely without hurting anything except her pride. But the photocopies were scattered about on the earth and cement. Worse, the dog had taken it into his head that this was a game and was now chasing several pages and batting them with his paws.

'Leave them alone, there's a good dog!' She tried to retrieve her papers, but the more she pulled at the one end of a sheet the more the dog tugged and ripped at it.

The big brute growled in a gruff way and seemed to laugh at her. She was about to give up the fight and go back into the library to do the photocopying all over again when a masterful voice gave a sharp order behind her.

'Heel, Brutus! Drop that!'

The order was given with such a deep tone of authority that Gabrielle and the dog both froze.

The dog obeyed instantly and bounded to the feet of a tall young man who had short-cropped black hair, a ruddy well-scrubbed face and bright grey eyes. Although he was thin he was well muscled.

'He didn't attack you, did he?' When the young man spoke to Gabrielle his voice was tinged with concern. 'He wouldn't normally misbehave and make a nuisance of himself. He's usually very obedient.'

'Oh, don't blame the dog.' She spoke up quickly in its defence as it sat looking cross and grumpy close to its master. 'It was all my fault. . .really. I dropped the papers on his head. I think he was asleep or snoozing. Please don't punish him.'

The young man eyed her closely, then looked relieved. Immediately he bent to pick up the torn shreds of paper, still on the ground. 'What a mess, Brutus,' he addressed the dog firmly. 'We'll have to make these copies over again.' He looked at Gabrielle. 'He's as good as a shredding machine. I'm sorry.'

'It can easily be redone.'

'You're shaking,' he said gently. 'Would you like to go in and sit awhile?'

'I'm fine. I'd just like to get the photocopies done.'

'I'll help you. After all, you wouldn't be in this mess if it wasn't for me. My name is Ivan Janowski, by the way. Please come and be formally introduced to my dog. If he knows you, you'll never have any trouble with him again, whatever the situation.'

Gabrielle did feel a little apprehensive in front of the dog, who had a half sulky look as if he wasn't sure whether he was in for a reproof or not.

'Brutus, hold up your paw for. . .' Ivan turned. 'I don't know your name.'

'Gabrielle Ford.'

'Shake hands with Gabrielle, Brutus. And never cause her any trouble again!'

The dog eyed his master, then held up his paw, and Gabrielle took it.

'He likes to be tickled behind his ears,' Ivan encouraged.

As Gabrielle slipped her fingers behind the short pointed ears the dog gave what could only be described as a contented grin. He certainly looked very docile. As she withdrew her hand Brutus pushed forward, eager for more.

Ivan laughed. 'You're good friends now. If you're ever in trouble, Gabrielle, and you see Brutus about, just call and he'll defend you.'

'Is it that dangerous here, then?' she asked incredulously.

'No. But with Brutus by your side you're as safe as the Crown Jewels.'

'I'm sure.'

'Let me help you with the photocopies, then if you like I'll take you for lunch.'

This unexpected invitation made Gabrielle stare up into his grey eyes. 'There's no need to——'

He broke in, 'I'd like to.'

It was settled. They went back into the library, but now the whole place was crowded out with students. The photocopying machines on the medical floor all had queues and there was nothing for it but to wait their turn.

Finally a machine was free. As Ivan pressed the button to make the first copy Gabrielle saw a glint of gold on one of his fingers. 'Quick—show me your ring?' She grasped his hand.

'Whatever's got you so excited?' he asked as she turned the ring around and examined it closely.

'Oh!' she exlaimed with disappointment.

'What did you think it was?'

'I thought it was a skull and crossbones, but it's only a buckle. But very handsome,' she added.

'Hmm. There's a story behind my ring,' Ivan said wistfully. 'But I doubt if it's as intriguing as yours.'

Gabrielle gave a brief summary of her accident and of her highway doctor while they continued with their task.

'That's a real mystery and imagination episode,' Ivan said. 'I can't ever remember any doctor around here wearing such a ring. I'll ask about, though. You've gone quite red and flushed, Gabrielle. He's still very important to you, isn't he?'

'Yes.'

'I wonder if you'll ever find him?'

Gabrielle ran all the way back to the clinic. It had taken an eternity to get Claudia's re-copying done. And because of all the hassle, Ivan had very sweetly invited her out for lunch later in the week.

When Ruby Pearly heard how Gabrielle had spent her lunch hour, she sniffed in disgust and set about preparing coffee and a snack of cheese and biscuits, while Gabrielle put the copies neatly on Claudia's desk.

Gratefully sipping her coffee, Gabrielle hoped the copies would be to Claudia's liking. Then the phantom of her thoughts appeared in the doorway of the staffroom.

Claudia spoke sharply. 'I want to see you in my office, Nurse Ford. . .immediately!'

Gabrielle followed her.

'Are you in love, Nurse Ford?' Claudia demanded the moment the door shut behind them.

The question shocked Gabrielle. But she had no time to give any sort of answer, for Claudia swept on. 'That's the only explanation I can think of for your shoddy and stupid actions!'

'I beg your pardon?' protested Gabrielle.

Claudia stood behind her desk, making the most of the barrier of the furniture. She held up the photocopies and slapped the top pages with her hand. 'You can't have your mind on the job. Whatever possessed you to make a copy of an article that's all in Japanese?'

'I thought it odd at the time, but the article was in exactly the place you'd written down.'

'Surely you could have used a little common sense? I expect there was an English translation after it.'

'No. . .no, there wasn't. I looked.' Gabrielle tried hard not to stumble over her words. She didn't want to give this woman the satisfaction of seeing her undermined in any way.

'There's always a translation in these journals.'

'I assure you there wasn't. Anyway, there's a summary in English at the beginning of the article.'

'Quite useless,' Claudia bit out, her colour rising and her green eyes sparking venom. 'A summary the length of a single paragraph can't possibly have the detail that I require.'

The argument only stopped when Eliot strode into the room and closed the door.

'What in God's name is going on in here? Even the patients can hear!'

That super-soft voice, so controlled and full of authority, sent a cold shiver down Gabrielle's spine.

CHAPTER FIVE

'ELIOT . . .this little nurse of yours hasn't an ounce of brain in her skull!' Claudia snapped angrily.

'I find that hard to believe. She's got enough grey matter in her brain to assist me quite capably.'

Claudia ignored his remark. Inwardly she raged because he hadn't taken her part. 'Just look at this!' She handed over the papers.

'I always think the Japanese have such beautiful handwriting. You could even frame this and hang it as a picture.' He sounded laconic.

Claudia was near bursting point. 'And that's about all it's fit for! How on earth am I supposed to know what all those squiggles mean?' She ranted on about the importance of the lecture she had to give in a week's time and how she liked to be well prepared. 'I need to have every iota of knowledge at my fingertips when I lecture those second-year med students. They all seem to be so slovenly nowadays, not at all like we used to be.'

Eliot had installed himself on her desk so that

he was between her and Gabrielle. 'I think you
can easily turn this mistake. . .' he shrugged his
shoulders '. . .into your advantage, Claudia.
You're always telling me that students don't
listen attentively enough. Get a photographic
slide made of this page, throw it up on the
screen at the beginning of your lecture. Tell the
students to make notes because they'll have an
exam question on the subject. Then start talking
gobbledegook in an Eastern accent. At first
they'll be horrified at the idea that they have to
take notes in Japanese. Then they'll see the
joke, and after they've all had a good laugh I'll
guarantee you'll have a captive audience.'

'Eliot, you're just brilliant!' cooed Claudia.
'Yes, of course. They'll think it was a joke and
they'll go about telling everyone how good I
was. Yes, yes, I'll really get myself noticed
then.'

Gabrielle caught Eliot's half-smile and wondered whose side he was on.

'Quite right, Claudia,' he continued. 'And
you always say if you want to get on you have
to get yourself noticed.'

'You're wasted here, Eliot,' she began again.
Mercifully it was as if Gabrielle didn't exist.
'But none of this is to the point. Nurse Ford
must have dragged some of these papers
through the gutter!' Gabrielle's respite hadn't

lasted for long; Claudia was on the attack again. She held out two papers for Eliot to inspect. 'Look here!' she gesticulated.

'You can still read the print. This dust is only on the back,' he pointed out. Turning to Gabrielle, he asked, 'Did you fall into a builder's work pit or something?'

'No, Dr Cougar—I tripped and fell, and the sheets went over some sand and cement. I'm sorry if they're dirty.'

He eyed her for a moment, then twisted around to Claudia. 'Are you satisfied? Or do you want them redone?' He sounded impatient.

Claudia caught his tone and backed off. 'I'm sure I'll manage, Eliot. And with your good advice I think I'll come up trumps.' She flashed him a radiant smile.

'In that case I'll take my little nurse away.' And he guided Gabrielle back to his office.

Gabrielle was in a state of suspended shock. She had not expected a row with Claudia, and furthermore she had not expected Eliot to protect her. Because that was exactly what he had done. It had been his flair and imagination that had turned the situation around and, outwardly at least, pacified Claudia.

Once inside his office he said, 'You must forgive Claudia—she likes things to be exact. And these lectures of hers are very important to her. She does a good job too. Please understand that she's a little too exacting at times.'

'I can understand that.' Gabrielle thought it best not to whip up the situation. And, after all, she was talking to Claudia's fiancé.

Eliot slipped his hand around the back of her neck and lightly traced his fingertips down her spine. 'No damage to your back, I hope?' he asked.

'My back?' His touch had sent an unexpected delicious shiver through her. She blushed.

'Yes, you said you fell. Did you jar your back at all?'

'No. . .no damage, thank goodness.' She wished he would not stand so close. His hand remained lightly in the hollow of her back. If only he'd take it away!

'That's all right, then. Good. Let's get on with the first patient.'

His actions and his touching concern had left her in a daze, and she struggled to bring herself back on to a plane of reality. For an engaged man his behaviour was far too intimate in some ways. This disturbed her much more than it should.

Fortunately the whole afternoon went by like a flash. They were busy. Mrs Grey had returned with her neck X-rays and a report from the radiologist. Everything was satisfactory. Eliot

referred her to Physiotherapy for further examination and treatment, and after she had left the
consulting-room he spoke to Gabrielle.

'I'm not at all sure about Mrs Grey. If she
returns from Physio with the same symptoms,
which I believe she will, I'm going to be at a
loss.'

'Shall I book her for a half-hour appointment
with you when she returns?' Gabrielle sug-
gested. 'Perhaps if you have a long talk with her
you'll be able to uncover something.'

'Good idea. I'll leave that to you.'

His smile was so disarming that she wished he
weren't so handsome. He was beginning to have
a definite effect on her. And the problem was it
wasn't at all unpleasant.

All afternoon Gabrielle worked well with
Eliot. He seemed surprisingly happy and even
whistled to himself in between patients.

'Who's my next patient, Nurse?' He gave her
a broad grin.

'Jim Duke.'

'Ah, the Duke himself. He's in a rock band.
It's not his thumb again, I hope?'

'I think it is,' replied Gabrielle. 'He's clutching it and it's swathed in cotton wool.'

Eliot stood up from his desk and sighed.

The Duke walked into Eliot's office in a regal
fashion. Gabrielle was impressed by his flashy

clothes. He wore a beautiful white suit, a black shirt with a mandarin collar and, at his throat, a chunky metal object that looked suspiciously like a car medallion from the bonnet of a Volkswagen. He took off his Panama hat with a flourish and Gabrielle saw his black hair tied neatly at the nape with a band of multi-coloured beads. He was definitely rock-'n'-roll material.

'It's happened again,' said the Duke forlornly, and held out his hand towards Eliot.

Eliot shook his head slowly. 'Sit down here and let me put a spotlight on it. Nurse Ford, remove the dressing with care, please.'

Gabrielle took her time to gently extricate the thumb. What she saw made her grimace inwardly, but her hospital training had drummed it into her never to show revulsion whatever the damage to the body.

With care, Eliot examined the thumb under the light. It was red and swollen and the skin was split very deeply down the pad. Red angry granulation tissue lay in a deep furrow; the surrounding skin did not cover it.

'Well, Duke,' he began slowly, 'we've been through all this before, and I told you. You know the old saying, "It'll never get well if you pick it", and this will never heal if you don't stop plucking with it.'

'Yes, Dr Cougar, but I've got to practise my

instruments and I've got to put in a lot of time on my guitar. You know the band is just taking off. We've done several gigs lately, and they've all been sell-outs. And when you've got a theatre full of fans all screaming for you you can't let them down.'

'I know you're doing great things with the band, Duke. My daughter tells me all about you.'

'She's a fan, is she, Doc?' The Duke looked as pleased as a pussycat with a bowl of cream. 'Just fix me up to play my guitar and I'll get her a front seat at my next gig, and she can come backstage after. You come too.'

'Could my eardrums stand the noise, Duke? And more to the point, could your thumb stand it?'

'Ah, come on, Dr Cougar, you can fix me up!'

'Can't you use a pick of some sort, Duke?'

'No good. To get my particular sound with the bass guitar I use a slapping motion—more like percussion of the strings. A plectrum wouldn't give the same effect.'

Eliot sighed. 'It's that perpetual slapping motion of the steel strings that's the cause. But, as you say, it's that technique that gives you your exclusive sound.'

Eliot left Gabrielle to clean the wound. The

Duke hadn't looked very hopeful at the prognosis. Eliot believed that daily dressings at the clinic, infra-red lamp treatment and a long rest would be the only cure.

Duke stared forlornly at his thumb as Gabrielle arranged his hand under the lamp for a twenty-minute treatment.

'It's dreadful not being able to play my instruments.' He sounded so dejected. 'Makes me feel like a man in the dole queue!'

'If you were a boxer your coach would tape your hands, Duke.' Gabrielle looked at the deep wound again. 'The way you play your guitar. . .well, it looks as though you put your thumb through as much punishment as if you were actually in the ring.'

Just then Eliot poked his head around the cubicle door. 'You've got it, Nurse Ford! The very treatment!'

'What's that, then?' Duke's eyes were shot with eagerness.

'Taping!' exclaimed Eliot triumphantly. 'Nurse Ford here is exactly right. Boxers have their hands taped before a bout, so that's what we'll do for you. Simple athletic tape around your thumb will give your skin that all-important protection.'

'Brilliant!' Duke grinned widely at Gabrielle. 'Your new nurse isn't just a pretty face, eh?'

Unexpectedly Gabrielle felt herself blushing. But it wasn't at Duke's outright wicked wink. It was at the trace of a smile that tugged at Eliot's mouth, and the warm way that his eyes sparkled as he said, 'We aim to please.'

Lunch with Ivan Janowski was a pleasant affair at a nearby Italian restaurant. It turned out that both he and Gabrielle were nursing broken hearts.

Ivan's long-standing girlfriend had taken up with another man shortly after a blazing row.

'It was a stupid quarrel,' Ivan said slowly as he sipped his coffee. 'I think I've lost Karen for ever now.'

Gabrielle tried to bolster his confidence and said she was sure that things would turn out all right.

Ivan shook his head. 'But I haven't forgotten my promise to you. I've asked all over campus about a doctor who wears a skull-and-cross-bones ring. I haven't any good news yet, but the network is large. And if he's anywhere in Canada we'll find him for you.'

Gabrielle munched her chocolate mint. 'Thanks, Ivan. My brother is in pre-med and he's put the word out through that grapevine too.'

They collected Brutus outside the restaurant

and Ivan and his dog walked Gabrielle back to the practice. Outside the glass door of the entrance they said their goodbyes.

'I bet you find your skull-and-crossbones doctor just as you fall in love with someone else,' grinned Ivan. 'Life's funny like that.'

Gabrielle thanked him for a lovely lunch and kissed him lightly on the cheek. Brutus jumped up and down in delight, so she gave him a special tickle behind his ear and they parted laughing.

As she entered Reception she saw Eliot going towards his office. He looked remarkably sour. She supposed he and Claudia had been arguing.

The afternoon was hectic. One patient after another tried to book an immediate appointment. Somehow she managed to fit them all in, but it was a tight squeeze.

Eliot had worked efficiently all the time concentrating on his patients. It was as if he hardly noticed Gabrielle.

The weather had taken a turn for the worse that afternoon. Instead of the bright hot sunshine that had bathed Ivan and Gabrielle at lunchtime, it was pelting with rain.

Jeremy ran up to the main entrance, shook himself dry and poked his head around the door. He saw his sister at the reception desk.

'Is it OK if I wait for you in here today, Gabrielle?'

'Of course.' She was pleased to see him. 'Just sit in the waiting area. I shouldn't think I'll be more than twenty minutes.'

Her brother hung up his drenched bomber jacket in the corner and settled himself on a hard chair with a book in his hand. It didn't surprise Gabrielle that it was one on genetics.

She walked up to him and said in a mischievous whisper, 'Your genetics professor must be ravishing! I only ever see you reading her textbooks.'

'Nonsense!' He tried to keep a serious face. 'I've finished all my other homework. But you're right—she is ravishing. And I'd like to be the one to ravish her.'

Hmm, thought Gabrielle. A crush on his professor won't do his marks any harm. She walked towards the reception desk again.

Ruby Pearly came up to her. 'Raining cats and dogs out there. . .and oh, look, here's a little kitten almost drenched in the downpour!'

Gabrielle turned to see Trish. Her hair was soaked and flat against her head and she clutched her chest as she shivered.

'Poor lamb, come with me,' cooed Ruby. 'I'll get you a towel to dry your hair and a little something to eat.'

'Great!' Trish ran around the counter. When she saw Gabrielle she slowed down to a walk and said very formally, 'Good afternoon, Nurse Ford.'

Eliot had obviously had a few stern words with his daughter, for she was on her best behaviour today.

'Hello, Trish. I'll tell your father you're here.' Gabrielle was mindful of Eliot's words the other day. He had stated very dramatically that whenever Trish came to the clinic he was to be informed straight away.

Eliot was talking on the telephone as Gabrielle quietly pushed the door open. 'This is Eliot Cougar here. . . Yes, from the 112th Street practice.' A short pause. 'Tell your supervisor that I want those blood sample reports straight away. Don't tell me you're busy. So is everyone. . .'

Gabrielle pitied the poor woman on the receiving end of this conversation. She knew from experience that Eliot in a temper was a formidable proposition. She stood just inside the doorway waiting for a suitable moment to interrupt.

He was barking into the mouthpiece again. 'The doctor's doing the lab tests himself? Good. I'll hold until he can give me a verbal report. . . Yes, that's what I said. I'll wait.'

Eliot looked up suddenly. 'Your daughter is here, Dr Cougar,' Gabrielle told him.

Immediately his face brightened. 'What's she doing with herself at the moment? I'm a bit tied up here.'

'She got soaked in the rain. Mrs Pearly has taken her off to dry her hair.'

'Good.' He nodded, then covered the mouthpiece of the telephone with one large hand. 'No doubt she'll give her something to eat as well.'

'Yes, I did hear something about nutty crunchies.'

'I hope Trish was polite to you, Nurse Ford?'

'Oh, yes, sir. She made a point of giving me a very formal "good afternoon".'

Eliot smiled. 'I should hope so too! I read the riot act to her about her little piece of mischief. It's all very well for her to play games with me at home, but not here. If she's with Mrs Pearly she can't come to much harm.'

Gabrielle excused herself and went away to tidy a cubicle.

It was some minutes later when she arrived back in the reception area. Jeremy had company. Trish had installed herself on the chair next to him and they were poring over some of Trish's books.

'Is my brother helping out with your homework?' Gabrielle asked.

Trish looked up and blushed. 'Is he your brother?'

'Yes. For better or worse.'

The girl smiled shyly.

'I'll leave you two to your plant studies.' Gabrielle smiled secretly to herself and went back to Mrs Pearly.

'Our Trish has found someone more her own age to talk to,' Mrs Pearly said. 'I'm glad. Your brother's good with kids, by the looks of things.'

Just then Eliot marched up to Reception. The intercom from one of the other doctors' offices buzzed and Mrs Pearly hurried away.

'Is my daughter still drying her hair?' Eliot asked.

'No, sir, she's studying.' Gabrielle pointed to Trish and Jeremy. They were absorbed in their talk, and neither noticed Eliot.

Eliot was suddenly tense. 'I can't leave my daughter alone with you for five minutes! Who the devil is that virile young chap she's latched on to? He's not one of my patients, is he?'

'No, sir——'

'Then whose patient is he? Dr Huntridge's?'

Gabrielle sensed another bout of trouble. 'He's not a patient——'

'Then what the hell is he doing here?'

'Waiting for me. He's my brother. I didn't think you'd mind—he's not doing any harm.'

'Virtually seducing my little girl! And she's only thirteen, you know.'

'He's doing nothing of the sort. He's only helping her with her biology homework.'

'Biology?' His face turned crimson. 'I'm her father. I'm the one to explain any biology to her.' His eyes glittered dangerously and his anger was all directed at Gabrielle. 'I want my child to learn about certain things from me. I don't want her learning the facts of life in a giggly, smutty way. I'll teach her about love and affection first.'

The man was mad. Completely over the top. Gabrielle looked him steadily in the eyes and said flatly, 'Jeremy is teaching Trish about photosynthesis—that's how a plant gets its food.'

'Oh!' Eliot looked one shade less furious. 'That's a relief.' He glanced over his shoulder at the pair again. 'And what's your brother studying?'

'He's in medicine, sir.'

'Medicine?' he bit out, keeping the volume of his voice menacingly low. 'Med students are the worst! It's human biology that they have on their minds all the time. And I know where that leads. To think there's even an anatomy book with pictures of Marilyn Monroe for surface markings! Then all they want to do is practise. Yes, definitely medical students are the worst!'

Gabrielle had had enough. Eliot wasn't going to attack her brother. 'If you say they're the worst then you should know, Dr Cougar. After all, you were a med student once—even though that must have been a very long time ago.'

He said nothing, just glared at her. Then, 'Am I to believe your brother is a paragon of virtue? Just tell him Trish is thirteen.'

'You're being ridiculous!' she bit back. 'Jeremy isn't interested in the Lolita type.' She hurried on, fearful that she might regret that choice of name. 'In fact he prefers older women, so your daughter is quite safe.'

'Your brother has an eye for the main chance, then?'

'Your reasoning is despicable, Dr Cougar! Actually it's one of his professors that he's rather fond of.'

'Who?'

'I don't have to tell you.'

Eliot relaxed a little and leaned close to her with his elbows on the counter. 'Pre-med student. Now, would that be the delectable Ann Stamp that your brother fancies?'

She did not answer, but he could see that he was right.

'Listen, Gabrielle. I know Ann, and your brother's heart is about to be broken. She's virtually engaged to a neurologist at the university hospital. Now if I promise not to tell your brother that heart-shattering piece of information, will you promise to have a subtle word with him and point out that Trish is very definitely under age?'

'That sounds like a most elegant piece of blackmail, Dr Cougar.'

'Yes. . . Do you agree?' He was smiling now. 'I think I've been acting the over-protective parent.'

'Something like that.' Gabrielle was relieved that Eliot had calmed down. She wasn't sure why he had changed track, but he had.

'I'll have a word with my brother tonight, Dr Cougar.'

He stretched out and clasped her hand. She was shocked. 'Please do, Gabrielle. And when I come to you for advice again call me Eliot.'

All her senses were jangling. It was with an effort that she said, 'Yes, Eliot. If you make a big thing about Trish and Jeremy, Trish will only want her own way more.'

'I'm sure you're right, Gabrielle. Looking into your sapphire-blue eyes has calmed me down and made me see reason. Now, introduce me to your brother.'

Gabrielle was pleased about one thing. If she had to introduce Jeremy, Eliot would have to loosen his hold on her hand. The physical effect he had on her was electric.

When the introductions were made Jeremy stood up and thrust the biology book back into Trish's hands. 'I'm very pleased to meet you, sir,' he said politely.

'It seems I must thank you, Jeremy,' Eliot began. 'If you've helped Trish with her home-work, it means I can have a quiet evening.'

'Oh, no, Daddy,' Trish interrupted. 'There's still English and French.'

Eliot put his hand round his daughter's shoulder and grinned. Gabrielle thought he made a good father, even if he was a little over-sensitive at times.

Eliot spoke to Jeremy again. 'You've got a long haul of study ahead of you before you get MD after your name. Don't forget that even your first-term marks will be scrutinised before you're accepted for med school. And even after that they'll remain on your transcript for ever.'

'Yes, sir, I know. I'm working hard right from the word go.'

Eliot eyed him from top to toe. Gabrielle was thankful that Jeremy was wearing a new sweater. When he studied he leant on his elbows and the sleeves of many of his old ones were threadbare.

'Have you any idea what you might like to specialise in yet, Jeremy?' Eliot went on.

'I'm not sure, sir. Not at this stage. But at the moment I'm very interested in genetics. Perhaps something to do with genetic research and genetic counselling.'

'Ah, so you'd like to be a high-flyer in medical science.' Eliot looked impressed. 'You want to be at the cutting edge of research. Very commendable. Mind you, a stint in general practice for a year or two, as a good medical grounding, wouldn't do you any harm.'

'No, sir.' Jeremy's eyes grew wide with disbelief. 'I'd like to do some general work before I decide.'

'Good.' Eliot pulled his daughter closer. 'I'll bear you in mind when you qualify. Oh, and I'll put in a word for you with Dr Stamp. We're old friends.'

What an about-turn! thought Gabrielle. And I thought he'd have it in for Jeremy. Instead, he's gone out of his way to be nice—more than nice.

Eliot made Trish say goodbye and took her away.

Jeremy stood stunned with his eyes unblinking. 'Did you hear that, Sis? He's going to speak to Dr Stamp about me!' He thrust his fist to his mouth. 'Oh, my God, my heart's beating like a rocket!'

'Wait for me here,' chuckled Gabrielle. 'Don't go into orbit without me!'

No one in the little group saw a shadowy figure walk stealthily back to her office. No one saw the woman doctor's door close quietly or her rigidly furious body as it leant there for a moment. And it was as well for Gabrielle that she did not see the green-eyed doctor's clenched fist bang down on her desk or the pile of patient files that were sent scattering to the floor.

On their walk home Jeremy was in a daze. 'You know, Gabrielle, there must be justice in the world,' he said happily. 'I gave that little kid a bit of help with her homework, and, out of that, the world has opened up for me. Do you really think Dr Cougar meant it when he said he'd consider me for a job?'

Gabrielle gulped. 'I doubt he'd have said so if he hadn't meant it.'

'And fancy him knowing Dr Stamp! I hope he does remember to mention me to her. I'd be in seventh heaven if she spoke to me. Isn't he fantastic. . .the Big Cat?'

Jeremy was certainly scudding along cloud-high. Gabrielle felt uncertain.

'Why do you call him the Big Cat, Jeremy?'

'Oh, everyone does—everyone on campus,

anyway. You know, I think he's right. I'll have to take my studies very seriously. It's nice coming home with you and having you cook and all that. But it might be better if I stayed on at the library with Brooker. He's always there until closing time—gets his food at the student canteen. It's good and pretty cheap there. And I think I've got enough of my money to see me through.'

Gabrielle was silent as she walked on. 'Yes, Jeremy, that's a good idea of yours. You'll have Brooker for company too.'

'Yes, he doesn't slouch off either. He does an hour of study, has ten minutes off to unfog his mind and then goes on to another subject.'

Gabrielle studied the pavement as they marched on. The Big Cat was a good name for Eliot. He was like a cat's paw, warm and furry, but with claws too. And how admirably he had manipulated Jeremy into doing just what he wished! Now Jeremy would no longer call in at the practice. He'd be in the library. It was unlikely therefore that he would ever see Trish again.

Eliot was as fascinating and dangerous as a cougar could be. She shivered. How cunning he had been to dangle those two precious prizes before Jeremy! Not only a mention to her brother's heart-throb, but the promise of a job.

And in this economic climate even doctors' jobs weren't as numerous as they had once been.

She felt her blood run cold. More disturbing than anything had been Eliot's attitude to her. There had been no necessity to hold her hand or make it plain that he had noticed the particular colour of her eyes. What was that all about? The man was full of trickery and deceit. His secret engagement to Claudia was just one proof of his cunning methods.

Discover
FREE BOOKS
AND
FREE GIFTS

From Mills & Boon

As a special introduction to
Mills & Boon Romances we will send you:

FOUR FREE Mills & Boon Romances plus a FREE
TEDDY and MYSTERY GIFT when you return this card.

But first - just for fun - see if you can find and circle four
hidden words in the puzzle.

R	D	A	V	R	Y	B	X	N	M
B	O	O	K	N	C	A	S	P	Y
Z	G	M	N	B	U	L	T	R	S
R	T	N	A	N	E	F	T	A	T
D	H	I	A	N	V	K	D	M	E
N	W	L	K	H	C	O	W	S	R
O	C	O	M	U	T	E	D	D	Y
I	L	V	F	L	P	B	I	T	E
F	E	E	J	S	G	I	F	T	P
S	P	N	S	E	T	I	N	R	E

**The hidden
words are:**

MYSTERY
ROMANCE
TEDDY
GIFT

Now turn over to claim your
FREE BOOKS AND GIFTS

Free Books Certificate

Yes! Please send me four specially selected Mills & Boon Romances, together with my FREE Teddy and Mystery Gift. I would also like you to reserve a special Reader Service Subscription for me. Which means that I can go on to enjoy six brand new Romances sent to me each month for just £8.70, postage and packing FREE. If I decide not to subscribe I shall write to you within 10 days. Any FREE books and gifts will remain mine to keep. I understand that I am under no obligation whatsoever - I can cancel or suspend my subscription at any time simply by writing to you. I am over 18 years of age.

4A1R

FREE TEDDY

MYSTERY GIFT

Mrs/Miss/Mr _____

Address _____

_____

_____ Postcode _____

Signature _____

Reader Service
FREEPOST
P.O. Box 236
Croydon
Surrey CR9 9EL

CHAPTER SIX

BY THE way Jeremy rushed into the apartment early one evening, Gabrielle knew that he must have his mid-term exam results.

He was beaming from ear to ear as he plonked a large brown paper carrier bag on the kitchen table. 'We're celebrating tonight, Gabby! No cooking for you. I got all eights and two nines!'

She was delighted and hugged him. 'Congratulations! I suppose we're eating your favourite Chinese dishes.' She laughed as she found the plates and cutlery.

'I got a nine in genetics!' He was eager to tell her all about it.

'I never doubted that.' She turned and caught the twinkle in his eyes. 'Your passion for your professor had your nose virtually glued to her textbooks.'

His eyes shone brighter as he said, 'And when Dr Stamp gave me back my paper, she said, "Ah, Jeremy Ford. Your sister works with Dr Cougar. . . I've heard some good things about you."'

Gabrielle's breath caught in her throat. That came as a surprise. Eliot had said that he'd put in a good word for her brother, but she hadn't believed him.

'And what was your other nine for?'

'Sociology.'

She stared at him as he was about to spoon fried rice on to her plate. 'I didn't think you were taking sociology this term.'

'I'm not,' he laughed. 'I just helped Brooker with a paper. It was nothing. I trotted out a few of the things Dad used to say, and I found him some references in the library. He got a nine for that paper.'

Gabrielle was glad the two lads had remained friends.

'He's a good mate, Brooker,' Jeremy went on. 'He's got me a job at Christmas.'

'Oh, no!' Gabrielle sounded definite. 'You're not working in the holidays.'

'Only packing customers' bags in the food hall of Wardwoods—the store where he models sometimes. Easy.'

In a way Gabrielle was glad. They needed the extra money because the rent had gone up. But this she had kept from Jeremy. She hadn't wanted to worry him while he was studying.

Then she smiled as she thought of Brooker. 'A mate who's a part-time male model is a very useful friend, I suppose. I wonder what he's like on the catwalk?'

'Damned clever, if you ask me. I've seen some of his photographs. He can look a real swank when he wants. But you'd never guess late at night when he's poring over his books.' Then very seriously he added, 'I shan't forget all his help. After all, he let you jump the queue when you were late for your interview. It's just such a long time before I'm qualified.'

Over the weeks Gabrielle found Eliot occupying more and more of her thoughts. He had put in a good word for Jeremy just as he'd said. So her admiration for him had grown. But not unreservedly. She was still wary of what she believed were his tricky ways.

Eliot was sitting at his office desk looking through his patient files.

'You've allowed half an hour for my consultation with Mrs Grey, haven't you, Nurse Ford?' he asked.

'Yes, Doctor. She's your next patient. Shall I show her in?'

'Just a moment,' he said thoughtfully. 'I've got the letter from her physiotherapist and she didn't find anything more wrong with her neck than I did. There's nothing physically wrong.' He leaned back in his chair. 'Gabrielle, sit by

me when I have my little chat with Mrs Grey.
Watch her closely and see if you can come up
with any bright ideas.'

'But I'm not a doctor!' She was both aghast
and flattered. Why didn't he ask Dr Huntridge?
She was far more qualified—but, all the same,
very cool with patients.

'I'd like a bit of woman's intution. And I
want you here.'

'Very well. Shall I show her in now?'

'Please. In here.'

Mrs Grey smiled with an effort and followed
Gabrielle into Dr Cougar's office.

Eliot got up and walked around the desk to
greet his patient. He pulled out the hard-backed
chair and watched her carefully. Standing
slightly behind and to her side, he said, 'Is that
comfortable enough, Mrs Grey?'

With a stiff movement she turned her whole
body towards him, swivelling her eyes more
than her neck. 'Thank you, Doctor.'

Gabrielle took the seat on Eliot's left and sat
quietly.

'Now, Mrs Grey, you've completed your
course of therapy.' He smiled reassuringly at
her. 'How does your neck feel?'

The patient leant forward slightly, her brow
puckered with fine lines of anxiety. 'Oh, it's
better, just a bit.' She sounded apologetic.

'How much of an improvement do you think you've gained?'

'Quite a bit,' she said uncertainly.

'On a scale from one to ten with zero as no pain and ten as unbearable pain how much do you feel the treatment has helped?'

Mrs Grey sat contemplating this mathematical proposal. 'Oh, I've never been much good at math. . .but—well, say four.'

Eliot nodded. 'You're about forty per cent better now?'

'Yes. My neck felt lovely when I was having the treatment, especially the neck and shoulders massage, but as soon as I left the department, the old headache started up again.'

Gabrielle watched as Eliot listened carefully. He seemed to be searching his patient's face for clues.

'Well, now, any improvement, however temporary, is better than none. How is your health generally?'

'Fine,' came the non-committal answer.

Eliot tried to pin Mrs Grey down by siting the individual systems of her body. 'Tummy all right?'

'Yes.'

'Chest all right? No pains or difficulty with breathing?'

'No problem, Doctor.'

He went on with what Gabrielle thought was an exhaustive list. 'Periods all right?'

'No problem.' She dropped her head. '*Mine* are fine.'

Gabrielle caught the inflection on the word 'mine'. She looked towards Eliot.

He had heard that too, and she saw his half-smile. 'Yours are all right, Mrs Grey. But someone else's aren't.'

She looked up, astonishment widening her well-made-up eyes.

He continued, softly but definitely probing, 'Then it's your daughter who has problems with her menstruation?'

'No. . .yes. The problem is she hasn't started them yet, and she's seventeen, Doctor! Everyone else in her class at school has started and she keeps asking me why. It worries me, Dr Cougar. You see, my husband and I tried for a child for years and when at last I became pregnant we were overjoyed. It was such a dreadful time, all that trying and all those tests. I just don't want there to be anything wrong with our daughter. It makes lovemaking a real chore.' She dropped her voice.

'Seventeen isn't too late for a young girl to start her period, Mrs Grey.' Eliot sounded sympathetic. 'Everyone has a different internal clock. Has your daughter seen a specialist?'

'Yes, several. And they all say the same as you. It's this waiting that gets me down. The uncertainty, and they can't find anything abnormal. They say she'll start when she's ready.'

'I can see your point.' He rubbed his forefinger across his upper lip. 'If the specialists say there's no reason to worry, then just relax. I can tell you from experience that your daughter will be more of a worry to you when she is menstruating!'

Gabrielle was reminded of Eliot's overprotectiveness towards Trish.

He continued seriously, 'Not only will she have to adapt to the nuisance of it all, but she'll have to cope with the changing of girlhood to womanhood.'

Mrs Grey was listening attentively. 'You've got a daughter, haven't you, Dr Cougar? Has she had trouble too?'

'My Trish is only thirteen. She's started, and I'm amazed—she's coped and adapted better than I think I would. But I don't mind telling you I'd rather she'd started later. Her body may be mature enough to carry and deliver a baby, but psychologically she's too young. And that's very worrying to a father.'

Doctor and patient were talking like two old gossips, but Eliot was uncovering facts. Facts that lay beneath his patient's headaches.

'There we are,' said Mrs Grey, half smiling and half desperate. 'If you're good parents there's always something to worry about.'

'Have you a photograph of your daughter, Mrs Grey?'

'Oh, yes.' She rummaged in her handbag and held one out for him.

'Ah, I see she gets her good looks from you.'

Mrs Grey laughed and looked slightly more relaxed.

Eliot held the photograph out to Gabrielle. It showed a girl in a leotard with her hair drawn back tightly into a severe bun. She looked very thin and her muscles were too sharply defined in her neck and upper arms.

'A ballet dancer, and a serious one. You told me that last time you visited,' Eliot said lightly.

'She's very good, Dr Cougar.' The mother's chest rose in pride. 'If she doesn't grow any taller she has a chance for the ballet school.'

'I think you've just told me your daughter's reason for amenorrhea.' Eliot looked pleased. 'And you know, Mrs Grey, it's very common in young girls in the ballet. You see how thin your daughter is?'

'Yes,' said the mother, 'she has to keep to a stringent diet.'

'Exactly. That, together with her tireless vigorous physical activity, combines to hold up her periods.'

'How can that be? I thought dancing kept people at a peak of fitness.'

Eliot drew in a breath. 'Your daughter is perfect for the stage and the ballet, Mrs Grey, but Mother Nature doesn't think she's perfect to start having babies yet, so she's turned the internal clock back a few years.'

Mrs Grey was listening very attentively now.

Eliot continued, 'This condition is very typical among young people who take part in extreme physical exercise and strive for the heights of perfection with the body. I've even heard of some ballet dancers who didn't start their periods until they'd passed their teenage years. And, even after that, with the continued vigorous lifestyle sometimes the periods are sketchy and not at all regular.'

'I believe you, Dr Cougar. I want to believe you. But how come you can tell me all this and no one else has? I've dragged my daughter from one specialist to another.'

'As a generalist I know you and your whole family very well,' he explained. 'The whole picture is extremely important in coming up with the correct differential diagnosis. A lot of consultants just don't have the time either.'

Eliot spent the rest of the consultation time reassuring Mrs Grey and pointing out to her that this anxiety had probably been a major factor towards her headaches. He advised her to continue with the general movement and relaxation exercises that she had been taught and he arranged for another appointment.

Mrs Grey left Eliot's office a happier and a more relaxed person.

'Well done, Gabrielle,' Eliot grinned at her.

'What for?' she asked.

'I saw you pick up the vital word in that consultation. The word that led to the uncovering of all that Mrs Grey frets about.' He looked thoughtful, then added, 'Family matters. And, by the way, congratulate Jeremy on his nine for his mid-term genetics exam.'

Her eyes flew wide open. How on earth had Eliot picked up that piece of information? She certainly hadn't told him.

He answered her thoughts. 'I was talking to Ann Stamp the other evening. She says Jeremy has a deductive analytical mind. It was a pleasure for her to mark his paper.'

'He'll be thrilled to hear that. He's worked so hard. And how is Trish?'

'Up to her usual tricks at home, the little monkey. She positively swooned over your brother for a week, then he was all forgotten. You know how it is with girls of that age; they have a different man in their dreams every night.'

Suddenly he looked serious. 'When you're more adult you realise that the same person in your dreams every night is a far more satisfying proposition.'

She saw his eyes dilate and his lips part slightly. What was he trying to say? Backing away, she walked into the door. 'I'll show your next patient in immediately,' she said hastily.

His laughing eyes only made her more embarrassed. If Claudia Huntridge had heard all those seductive allusions, then Gabrielle's life would have been made a torment.

'Eliot, you're the limit!' Gabrielle heard Claudia castigate her boss as she approached his office after lunch.'

When Claudia sounded like this it was better not to interrupt. She stood hovering in the corridor waiting for the argument to conclude.

'I'm sorry, Claudia,' Eliot sounded irritable. 'I thought you said the lecture was earlier. I haven't arranged for anyone to be with Trish.'

'Well, find a babysitter, then. If it wasn't for the fact that your old housekeeper has been away so much lately we wouldn't be having all this trouble. For God's sake, a grown man like you, Eliot—you should have a late night out once in a while.'

'Where shall I find someone suitable at this late stage?'

'Don't worry, I'll fix it up.' The door of Eliot's office flew open and Claudia stepped into the corridor. 'Here! Here you are, Eliot. I'm sure your Nurse Ford wouldn't mind standing in at the last moment.'

She grabbed Gabrielle by the elbow and propelled her into the office.

And so it was that Gabrielle found herself agreeing to baby-sit for Trish that evening. She had been literally pushed into the situation and Eliot hadn't argued the toss. In fact he had looked pleased.

Because of the short notice Gabrielle didn't return to the apartment. Instead she ate supper with Jeremy and Brooker in the student canteen.

Brooker looked as tired as Jeremy, but there was something more; his fine features were pinched as if he was taut and in pain. But he ate his food like a horse, so she didn't think there could be much wrong with him. When he could relax after the exams he would be fine.

The drive leading to Eliot's house was long and dark. A small orchard of old apple trees stood like sentinels to her left. They were bare and black, now it was winter, and they looked like skeletons. A light wind tossed their thin branches and they appeared to wave her towards the yellow welcoming lights of the house. She was not afraid.

When Eliot opened the front door to her he said, 'I didn't hear your car drive up, and Trish has been listening.'

'Hello!' shouted Trish, and hung on to her father's arm.

Gabrielle greeted them both warmly. 'I haven't got a car. I walked.'

A darkness glazed his eyes. 'Never do that again—not on your own. Trish and I would have come to pick you up, wouldn't we?' He looked down at his daughter.

'Oh, yes,' she agreed happily with a lovely smile.

The vestibule was large and contained a beautiful oval mahogany table laid out with silver in the most exquisite taste. Gabrielle hardly had time to look around as she was whisked into the dining-room through a door on her right. It was small and cosy and very warm.

'You'll need a cup of coffee or something,' Eliot said. 'It's cold out tonight and slightly damp.'

The air was damp and cold. It had curled Gabrielle's hair into soft corkscrews that were very flattering and natural.

From the kitchen Eliot called sternly, 'Trish! Where's the rest of that seedcake and the angel cake with the yellow icing that I particularly like?'

The girl squirmed on her seat and said, 'There was hardly any left.'

'Not much. . .only half the seedcake and the whole of that angel concoction. Now there's nothing in the fridge but crumbs!'

'Oh, the butter must have eaten it.' Trish tried to laugh.

'Not funny this evening, little girl.' He advanced and bent close over her. 'Even if the butter is fat enough.' He stood up and said with a shrug of his shoulders, 'I'm sorry, Gabrielle—will plain Rich Tea biscuits do with your coffee?'

'That's all I really want—honestly.'

He returned to his task in the kitchen, but not without giving Trish a stern look.

As soon as he was out of earshot Trish asked, 'How's Jeremy?'

I haven't been in this house five minutes, thought Gabrielle, and already I'm on thin ice. 'He's very busy with his studies,' she answered.

'Oh, and I bet he gets high marks.' This little girl hadn't forgotten Gabrielle's brother.

'Yes.'

Trish sidled up to her. 'Has Jeremy got a steady girlfriend?' she asked.

Oh, dear, thought Gabrielle, now we're getting to the nitty-gritty! 'Yes, Trish.' She thought it best to bend the facts. She thought of Ann Stamp and said, 'He's very fond of someone.'

'Oh. . .' Trish looked crestfallen. 'I suppose she's older than me. It's not fair!'

'Yes, she is older.' Much older, thought Gabrielle. Thank goodness Eliot had appeared with the coffee. The topic would cease while he was present.

A knock on the front door sounded imperiously.

'She's early.' Trish drew her arms tightly into her sides and appeared to shrink within herself.

'I'll let Claudia in.' Eliot turned to leave. 'Odd—I thought I had another half-hour at least.'

Claudia's loud greeting and the obvious silence that told of their kiss made Gabrielle feel as uncomfortable as Trish looked.

Holding Eliot's arm rather too possessively, Claudia entered. She was wearing a mink that glistened under the lights. She looked seductive.

'So here you all are—nice and cosy! So kind of you, Gabrielle, and at the last minute too. Hello, Trish. How's school?'

'Fine.'

Claudia turned directly to Eliot. 'Really, darling, you're still in a shirt and no tie! Where's your jacket? No one would believe we were going out to a formal occasion. You look as though you're all set for a quiet evening in.'

'I'll go and get changed now.'

Trish jumped up. 'I'll help you to choose your shirt and tie, Daddy.'

Claudia installed herself in a seat opposite Gabrielle at the round table. 'He spoils that child!' she said sharply with a sneer. 'Eliot's too soft with her by far.' She gave a tinkling laugh. 'Still, it won't be long now. I'll be mistress here—then we'll see changes.'

Gabrielle didn't doubt that. There was an awkward lull in conversation. For no reason at all she found herself thinking of her skull-and-crossbones doctor. She asked Claudia if she knew anyone who wore such a distinctive ring.

For a split second Claudia paled, then recovering herself quickly she spoke in a drawl. 'Whatever sort of a doctor would wear anything so gauche? How tacky! I've certainly never seen anyone I know wearing such an object.' She moistened her lips. 'Why do you ask?'

'Oh, no reason.' Gabrielle felt a shiver of hostility emanate from the other woman, and she was glad when she stood up to receive Eliot again. He looked severe yet handsome in his charcoal-grey suit, and his features matched his clothes.

'We shouldn't be too late,' he whispered to Gabrielle after he had kissed Trish goodbye.

When the front door had closed Trish sat miserably in her chair. 'I hate her! She's a cold cow.'

'I've heard of a cold fish, but never a cold cow.' Gabrielle tried to sound light.

'She's a cow and she's cold. She doesn't really love Daddy—it's his money and his position in society that she's after. People think I'm too young to do most things, so I wouldn't know. But I watch, and I can tell everything.'

Gabrielle's heart went out to Trish. She might be young, but she thought she was right about Claudia.

Trish went on, 'Daddy's clever, but he doesn't see through her. I don't know why.'

Gabrielle believed she knew why. If Eliot and Claudia were to be married, then it was love that made him blind. Silently she agreed with Trish.

'And I hope she goes away on her own this Christmas,' Trish chattered on. 'Last year she came with us on a skiing holiday. I'm not that good and I don't like it. But Daddy was so keen.'

'Why? Don't you like snow?'

'Oh, yes, I love it. It's just that I'm hopeless on skis. I want to go in a straight line, but somehow I veer off to one side. And if I fall, I can't seem to balance properly and get up.' Trish looked miserable.

'But there are lots of other things you can do in the snow.'

'Yes, and I think Daddy would have. But Claudia wasn't keen. She kept laughing at me and calling me stupid and uncoordinated.'

It was easy to imagine Claudia trying to make herself out as superior to the poor child. Gabrielle's blood burned.

Later, as they sat playing cards, Trish said, 'Do you like Bela Lugosi?'

It was fortunate that Gabrielle had seen a late-night horror show the previous Saturday on the television—a 1931 black and white movie entitled *Dracula*.

She racked her brains. 'Isn't he the dark Hungarian who says "I am Dracu-la"?' The very name sent a shiver down her spine.

'You know him. My number one hero.' Trish stood up and said very importantly, 'You may come upstairs to my bedroom.'

Above the portal of Trish's door was a sign, white on black. 'Abandon hope all ye who enter here'. She pointed to it and said, 'Daddy put that there because he thinks I'm so untidy.'

Inside the room the walls were covered in huge posters, mostly on the horror movie theme—ghouls, goblins, Frankenstein monsters and all manner of weird beasts plastered the walls. How anyone could sleep peacefully in this room Gabrielle did not know.

'Here he is!' Trish pointed proudly to a black and white poster with Bela Lugosi in full regalia. 'And here and here and. . .'

The telephone shrilled. 'That's Amy—she said she'd phone. Excuse me, I won't be long.' And Trish dashed out.

To get rid of the feeling that she was in a monsters' den Gabrielle concentrated on the masses of books that ran along the side of the room. There was some comprehensive reading here, and she didn't notice the time until Trish came back.

'Sorry to have taken such an age,' she apologised. 'Amy does go on.'

'These are very good.' Gabrielle indicated the books.

Trish misinterpreted the gesture and said, 'Yes, Daddy made those shelves. And do you know, there's a really spooky story behind them——'

The telephone interrupted them for the second time and again Gabrielle was left. When

Trish returned she forgot to finish the spooky story about the shelves.

'Daddy's a great help with homework and things, but he can't do everything,' she explained.

Was Trish asking for help on a more personal level? Gabrielle wondered.

'I've got needlework tomorrow and I'm supposed to have this shift dress hemmed up. . .but I can't ask Daddy to get down on his knees. Somehow I don't think that's right.'

Suddenly the image of Eliot on his knees came into Gabrielle's mind. It was obvious he adored Trish and would never dream of doing anything to hurt her. Why then had he chosen Claudia as stepmother material? Perhaps his heart ruled his head.

'Yes, of course I'll help you, Trish.' And Gabrielle collected the pins and knelt on the thick bedroom carpet and slowly made her way around as she pinned up the hem.

Something was wrong. In order to make the dress straight on Trish she was having to take up much more hem on the one side than on the other.

'Are you standing up straight, Trish?' she asked. She looked up. The girl was looking at herself in the full-length mirror of the wardrobe.

Her monsters posters stared ghoulishly back at the reflection.

Standing up slowly, Gabrielle stood behind the little girl and to her horror saw the telltale signs. Her neck was shorter on one side than the other, and one shoulder was higher.

Pretending to straighten the material of the bodice at the back, Gabrielle ran her hands along one shoulder-blade, which stuck out like a fledgeling's wing. A cold wave ran through her. These signs all added up to the orthopaedic condition of scoliosis, a condition in which the spine curved to the side and the individual vertebrae rotated on top of one another.

'When you look like that, you look like I do sometimes,' Trish interrupted the pessimistic thoughts.

'Do I?' Gabrielle struggled to look normal and relaxed.

'Yes. I do think we look alike.'

Gabrielle finished the hemming but said nothing more to Trish. She was agonising over how she would tell Eliot.

Just as they were leaving the bedroom Gabrielle noticed two horizontal marks on the edge of the door. They had dates written above them.

'Is this some kind of growth chart?' she asked.

'Yes. Daddy measures me with a book on top

of my head. He's done it on my last two birthdays.'

Gabrielle studied the spacings. 'My, you have shot up in height during the last year!'

Downstairs in the kitchen Trish made hot chocolate with baby marshmallows floating on the top. It tasted a bit too sweet for Gabrielle's liking, but she drank it all the same.

Fortunately there was no need for much more conversation. Trish was tired, and after watching TV for half an hour she went to bed.

Alone in the big sitting-room, which was twice the size of her and Jeremy's flat, Gabrielle watched the minutes pass slowly by. It was important that Eliot be told as soon as possible. Scoliosis was a serious condition. If left untreated it could progress so far as to crush the vital organs of the chest, the lungs and the heart.

The sound of a car pulling up on the loose gravel outside and crunching footsteps put Gabrielle immediately on the alert.

Claudia looked smug. She had kept Eliot out much later than he had intended.

After the usual formal greetings he made his way to the drinks cabinet. 'Gin and tonic for you, Claudia?' he asked.

'As usual, darling.'

'What about you, Gabrielle?'

'Oh, just a soft drink.' She was nerving herself up to tell him.

'Orange juice like me.' He smiled as he handed her the thick-cut crystal tumbler.

'I'd like to speak to you about something personal concerning Trish,' Gabrielle began.

'Fire away,' he said, sipping his drink.

Gabrielle hesitated.

'I'm virtually family; you can talk in front of me,' Claudia interjected.

Gabrielle took a deep breath. 'Eliot, I think she's got scoliosis.'

'What are you talking about!' He spoke sharply. 'My little girl is perfect.'

'Such nonsense!' Claudia got up and sat on the arm of Eliot's chair. 'Take no notice, darling.' Then, addressing Gabrielle, 'How can you possibly tell? I wasn't aware that you'd attended medical school.'

To parry the sharp attacks Gabrielle said, 'I've attended many school screening clinics for scoliosis.'

'Poof! Now you're an expert.' Claudia waved a dismissive hand elegantly.

Gabrielle ignored this. 'When I was pinning up a hem for Trish I found it was much shorter on one side.'

'Are you sure the problem wasn't in your

inability to use a tape measure?' Eliot's eyes were fired with wrath.

Gabrielle listed the other signs of scoliosis, and the fact that Trish was growing rapidly now.

'I'm going up—right now,' Eliot said decisively.

Claudia tried to restrain him, but he shook her off roughly and made for the door.

Fiercely Claudia turned on Gabrielle. 'And what exactly do you hope to gain by this? You'll rouse his anger, nothing else.'

'Trish needs treatment.'

'She's a lazy little adolescent who slouches, that's all. If Eliot was firmer with her, made her take a few ballet lessons or something, she wouldn't look such a mess.'

Gabrielle was shocked by the brutal words and tone of the woman doctor.

They sat in silence while Claudia made herself another drink.

Much later Eliot came swiftly down the stairs. Without entering the sitting-room he called roughly, 'Gabrielle! Get your coat!'

'You see?' Claudia leaned forward, a malicious purr to her voice. 'You're in trouble now.'

Eliot was indeed black with anger. They drove the quick way home to Gabrielle's apartment and way above the speed limit. He halted his Volvo with a jolt, then turned to face her.

'You were right.' That was all he said, and the full significance of his words echoed inside the car.

'You didn't drag the poor child out of bed to examine her at this time of night, surely?'

'For God's sake, woman, I had to be a lot more subtle than that!' He was quite vicious-sounding. Then he spoke in a slow heavy voice. 'No. I went into her bedroom and sat on the bed. She was awake but sleepy, but I didn't care. I pulled her up into a sitting position and pretended to give her a big hug. She just thought I'd missed her this evening.'

He was leaning forward, his arms resting on the steering-wheel. The darkness of the night seemed to close in upon them.

He continued slowly, 'I ran my hands down her back and, yes. . . I felt the rib hump. . .'

Gabrielle knew she had been right. The spine of the scoliotic rotated and forced the ribs to do the same, so that they hunched up on the one side.

'It was the hardest thing I've ever had to do in my life. I had to say nothing. I had to keep control and pretend all was well.'

He sighed as he spoke, such a deep and protracted sound that Gabrielle instinctively put her hand out and held his as it lay on the steering-wheel.

'I wish with all my heart that it could have been otherwise,' she said.

Eliot sat up straighter, pushing himself with his hands against the wheel. It looked like a mighty effort.

Very gently he stroked the side of Gabrielle's face. 'If it hadn't been for you and your eagle eyes, this dreadful thing might have gone unnoticed for a long time.'

She made to hold his hand, but he withdrew it and started a long tirade on how he should have noticed the deformity. 'I can't understand how I missed it. And in my own daughter! How could such a thing have happened? And I pride myself on being a good doctor!' He thumped the dashboard with his fist.

'Don't blame yourself, Eliot. You haven't been with Trish for very long.'

'For eighteen months,' he grated. 'Long enough.'

'Sometimes these conditions are only really noticeable when adolescence starts anyway. Have you taken her swimming lately?'

'No. She doesn't like sport much.'

'Then you would never have seen her virtually undressed. And I'm not so sure that she isn't aware of something herself and has tried to hide it.'

'Why do you say that?'

'At thirteen she'll be growing into her young woman's body, and she'll be very aware of all the changes. I notice she likes baggy tops, not the skimpy ones. Even some of the photographs in her bedroom where she's with you in the summer show her in baggy outfits. She's probably chosen them on purpose, as a cover-up.'

'How observant you are, Gabrielle.' Eliot looked at her in amazement. 'I thought I could be both mother and father to her. But you see things that would never have entered my head.'

'I see with a woman's eyes.'

He was pondering. 'For two pins I'd ring up the orthopod from the university hospital who specialises in scoliosis and get him out of bed right now.'

Gabrielle raised her eyebrows.

'I know,' Eliot said solemnly, 'it wouldn't do any good at this late hour and I'd have to explain things to Trish first. I'll need to think carefully about that.'

The distracted look on his face softened slightly. 'However, you're still in my charge now, Gabrielle. I'd better see you safely indoors. That, at least, is the easiest task I can do tonight.'

They were silent as he walked her into the apartment building and up the small hallway on her floor.

Outside her door he took her face in both his hands. 'I had so many things planned. But this problem with Trish must be sorted out first . . .thank you for everything.' He kissed her cheek lightly and then ran his thumb across her lips before he kissed her with an infinite sweetness.

Her heart began to bound and all her pulses raced. Her cheeks and lips felt aflame at his touch.

She looked deeply into his dark sad eyes. The way her body was reacting was intense. She might have just received the kiss from her skull-and-crossbones doctor. She might be in love with this man.

But on his face she saw the pain of Trish's trouble deeply etched. And in nursing training she had been taught never to confuse love with pity. They were two strong emotions.

So, alone in her bed that night, she concluded that it was only pity that she felt for Eliot.

CHAPTER SEVEN

'THAT deep trough of a wound has completely healed.' Gabrielle was studying Duke's thumb under the spotlight in the treatment cubicle.

'It looks perfect to me. Surely it's time for the Big Cat to teach me about the taping, so that I can get back to my guitar?'

The Duke had attended regularly for his treatment, but now he was eager to get back into the swing of things. Several of his rock concerts were tentatively lined up.

'I'll find him for you now,' Gabrielle told him. 'It'll be up to him to give you the go-ahead.'

The Duke gave her a big wink.

She found Eliot in his office, his hand resting lightly on the telephone. He was looking pensive. But as soon as she told him about Duke's thumb he became his complete professional self. No one would have guessed the heartache that he must be feeling about Trish, and Gabrielle admired him tremendously for this.

'Beautifully healed, Duke,' Eliot agreed. 'And now for the taping.'

Gabrielle had found the roll of thin padding

125

material and the correct size of athletic tape. Eliot took time and care instructing Duke.

'You see, you just lay the tape on the part. Never wind it round like a coil of a tight spring; that could cut off the circulation.'

When the tape job was finished Duke flexed his thumb and played an imaginary guitar in the air. 'Great! It works a treat. And I've still got the flexibility.'

'That's because it hasn't been necessary to tape over the top joint of your thumb,' Eliot explained.

The Duke looked wonderingly at both of them.

'And the idea was so simple. Thanks. That's real rock-'n'-roll!'

'The best ideas are usually the simplest.' Eliot and Gabrielle shook hands with Duke and he left them, whistling.

As Gabrielle cleared away the hand table and replaced the taping material on the shelves Eliot sat on the plinth. She was acutely aware of how he watched her every move.

'I don't suppose you've had time to talk to Trish about her back?' Gabrielle asked gently.

'No.' He spoke quietly. 'I'll have to choose my words and my timing very carefully. . . Of course, this morning she's full of all the fun you had together last night. I hear you were even let into that inner sanctum of her bedroom.'

When he looked at her with those smiling steadfast eyes she felt her heart lurch, and she knew then that it wasn't pity that she felt for Eliot, but pure physical attraction.

'Yes.' She smiled at the idea of all the monsters on Trish's bedroom wall.

He continued very seriously, 'I've just rung the head orthopod's office at the university hospital. Professor Straitman specialises in scoliosis.' He looked down at his hands. 'Unfortunately he's in London, England, for a few weeks. But I've got Trish an appointment with him as soon as he's back.'

'I've heard great things about Professor Straitman from my brother,' she told him. 'Trish will have the best possible treatment, I'm sure.'

'Talking of treatments, we'll be short-staffed for a while here. Claudia has gone away to New York for another conference. I've arranged for a locum, but I imagine we'll be able to cope.'

Gabrielle couldn't understand why Claudia had left Eliot at this time. Surely he needed support and help with Trish? Their relationship was a mystery to Gabrielle. If she were Eliot's fiancée, Gabrielle would be with him all the time, conference or no conference.

After lunch with Ruby Pearly Gabrielle walked to the nearby pharmacy to buy some toiletries.

A sudden ear-piercing noise broke into her thoughts. It was the barking of a dog, and it was frantic and vicious.

Hurriedly she followed the sounds until she came to within sight of the commotion. An ambulance was present and men were clustered around shouting instructions, then swiftly running away. One man stood his ground. It was Eliot Cougar.

Gabrielle could see more clearly now. Brutus was standing over his master and defying any man to come near. The slumped body of Ivan Janowski lay inert on the ground. He must have stumbled on an uneven paving stone and knocked himself out with an unlucky landing.

Eliot held his coat in front and was trying to throw it over Brutus. She heard him yell to the ambulancemen, 'Hasn't the vet arrived? I need some kind of gun with a hypodermic dart to sedate this beast.'

'Leave Brutus alone!' Gabrielle cried. 'He's only trying to protect Ivan!'

Eliot swung round sharply. 'Don't be a fool, Gabrielle. Stay back. The dog will rip your throat out.'

'How badly is Ivan injured?' she cried desperately.

'I can't tell—I can't get near enough. There's blood under his head. I hope to God it's not coming from inside his ear.'

A sign of internal bleeding from the skull— Gabrielle knew that.

'Get all these men to stand back, they're only frightening poor Brutus,' she said. 'I'll calm him down and examine Ivan myself.'

Eliot narrowed his eyes and said, 'Of course, you know these two, don't you?'

'Let me try,' she pleaded.

'All right,' he ground out. 'It's against my better judgement, though.'

She called to Brutus again and again. But all he did was bark and lunge with his teeth bared.

'Try not to smile,' commanded Eliot. 'He'll interpret that as an aggressive gesture.'

Gabrielle tried again, and this time she bent down slightly. 'Good dog, Brutus. Come here— come here. Let me help Ivan.'

No good. Brutus barked more wildly. Then he leaped forward. Gabrielle saw Eliot lift a brick in the air. But all was well. Brutus ran whimpering to Gabrielle and buried his face in her hands.

She stroked the poor dog's head and whispered, 'Come and show me Ivan. I must see to him.'

As if in response Brutus led the way, and Gabrielle was able to examine Ivan. 'It's not from his ear,' she called to Eliot. 'The blood is from a gash on his cheekbone.' She examined his eyes, but they did not respond. He was out cold. . .unconscious.

With a firm hand on Brutus's thick leather collar, Gabrielle was able to keep him under control while Eliot and the rest of the ambulance crew lifted Ivan on to a stretcher and put him aboard.

Inside the ambulance was crowded. There was no room for anyone else but the patient, the ambulanceman, Gabrielle and, of course, Brutus, whom no one had the nerve to exclude. Eliot stood at the back of the vehicle. 'Don't bother to come back to the practice, Gabrielle,' he told her. 'Take all the time you need.'

The door closed, and the vehicle drove away along the main road. Eliot slung his coat over his shoulder and with head down walked determinedly back to work.

As they were transferring Ivan into Emergency he opened his eyes and flickered them.

'Wake up, Ivan,' Gabrielle said softly.

Brutus nudged his head against his master's side and made a funny soothing sound. Ivan managed to push his hand towards his dog, then he half turned and said faintly, 'Is that you, Karen?'

Gabrielle was, pleased to see Ivan coming back to consciousness. He was still not fully aware of all his surroundings, but the signs looked hopeful. She knew Karen was the name of his former girlfriend, and while she waited in Reception with Brutus she determined to give her a ring.

It wasn't hard to locate her telephone number; it was in Ivan's wallet. So Gabrielle gave her a call at work.

Karen had a pleasant-sounding voice. After the accident had been explained she said she would come straight away.

Brutus recognised her as she entered the emergency waiting-room. He danced for joy, and Gabrielle laughed. She was aware that Brutus knew his master's preference in women.

Ivan was admitted and it was decided that he should spend a day or two in hospital undergoing tests. But they were all routine; nothing to worry about.

Karen went up to the ward to settle him in while Gabrielle waited with Brutus.

Much later when the girl returned she said, 'I can't thank you enough, Gabrielle. We've made it up. I've decided to move in with Ivan when he's discharged. He was right about a lot of things.'

She took Brutus home with her, so Gabrielle was free to return to work.

'I didn't expect to see you back today.' Eliot looked concerned.

'Ivan has come round. There was no serious damage. His skull X-ray checked out OK, and he's conscious.'

'Thanks to you,' Eliot said softly. He was staring into her blue eyes. 'You were very brave. Where's the dog now?'

'Oh, I've seen to that,' she said absently. Suddenly she felt very tired. The excitement of the whole ordeal was catching up on her.

'Go home and rest, Gabrielle. There's nothing much to be done here this afternoon. I can manage.'

But Gabrielle stayed to help at the practice. She wouldn't let Eliot down.

The afternoon patient load was heavy. So it was already dark outside when Gabrielle was finally ready to leave. She and Eliot alone remained at the practice.

In Reception he waited for her, so that he could lock up. He looked exceptionally handsome muffled against the weather in his greatcoat and his hat. As she walked up to him she had to stifle a smile.

'What's amused you, Gabrielle?'

She wasn't sure if he was aware of the fact or not. 'Did you mean to start a new trend in hatbands?' she laughed.

He took off his black Homburg and surveyed it. 'Trish—the little monkey! Wait till I get home! I might have walked all through the streets with mistletoe in my hat. . .' He stood surveying the white round fleshy berries for a long time, then solemnly replaced his hat.

'It's rather early for Christmas decorations, Christmas is weeks away.' There was a sparkle in his eyes.

Gabrielle looked up into his big brown eyes. They were black with desire.

'Old Christmas customs. . .' he drawled slowly. 'They ought not to be allowed to die out.'

He took her in his arms and kissed her mouth, then slowly slid his rough cheek against hers.

Caught up in a heady desire for him, her mind suddenly reeled back in time. It was the brush of that rough cheek against hers. She was floating and hazy and all her senses were out of control. Momentarily she was not at the practice, not in Eliot's arms, but on the ground under the protective body of her skull-and-crossbones doctor.

She heard the blast again as if the car were

exploding, and as if in response she gripped Eliot firmly around his neck and kissed him with an ardour that had never possessed her body before.

Then she was being kissed back, and with such a fierceness that her whole body burned alive. She was not aware of how long their passion lasted. Time was standing still. But was she in the present or in the past?

Firm hands held her away, and Eliot's husky voice broke her dream and shot her into the present. 'How strange! I got the distinct feeling that we'd done that before. . .or something very like it.' He was breathing heavily. She stood shakily, almost being supported by him. 'Have we met before, Gabrielle? I mean. . .before you came here to work?'

The shock of the flashback and the intense reality of Eliot in a state of controlled arousal made her falter as she spoke. 'No, I don't think so.'

He looked steadily into her eyes, then slowly took his hat off. With a delicate touch he eased the sprig of mistletoe from the entrapping hat-band. After he had replaced his hat he found his wallet and placed the mistletoe carefully inside next to a photograph of his daughter. 'I'll have no further use for this,' he told Gabrielle with an infinite caress to his voice. 'After all, it's the quality of the kiss, not the quantity, that counts.'

She was still vibrating inside her very heart. Confusion more than anything reigned uppermost in her thoughts. She loved Eliot, but the memory of the skull-and-crossbones doctor was something else.

'I wish you a happy Christmas, Gabrielle. I'm sure all your future Christmases will be good ones.'

After she had said goodbye, Gabrielle walked home through the falling snow. It was a light shower; the individual flakes melted as soon as they touched the pavement before her feet. Am I seeing stars, she thought, or is this only cold melting snow?

CHAPTER EIGHT

WHEN Mrs Grey walked into Eliot's office she looked a different woman. She beamed and walked and moved with light easy movements.

'Nice to see you looking so happy,' he began.

'Oh, life is wonderful, Dr Cougar!' His patient was radiant. 'My daughter has started her periods. I'm so happy!'

Eliot nodded. 'Mother Nature took her time but came up trumps in the end.'

'Well, it was like this,' Mrs Grey told him. 'She grew and grew—too tall for the ballet, so she dropped it. Then she ate more, and within a few weeks she'd put on pounds and the periods started.'

'That's good,' Eliot grinned. 'And your neck?'

She laughed. 'No problem. I can't remember the last time I had a headache, and I can move any way I want.' She demonstrated. 'You see, Dr Cougar?'

'Very good. Very good.'

'It was the tension, I think.' Mrs Grey gave her own analysis. 'When my daughter's problem resolved itself the headaches went. And do you know what? My average in school is higher!'

Mrs Grey had her end-of-term results early because she had taken a night course. Gabrielle thought of Jeremy, whose results would be any time now.

'Congratulations,' Eliot said, then did a thorough examination. 'You're absolutely fine. You don't need my help any more.'

'You were such a strength to me, though, Doctor. I believed what you said, and it was that information that got me through the toughest stages.'

Mrs Grey thanked him again, then left.

Turning to Gabrielle, Eliot said, 'If only all our problems were as easily solved. I'm very glad. I didn't want to send her for a check-up from the neck up.'

Gabrielle had never heard that medical expression before. 'What does that mean?'

'I didn't want to send her to a psychiatrist. If you can pinpoint the underlying cause of the stress, the physical problems are easily understood.'

Gabrielle thought Eliot was a wonderful doctor, and she knew she loved him for more than his clinical expertise.

* * *

Dozing peacefully in bed, Gabrielle opened one eye and looked at the clock. She had a half-day off this Monday morning, as Eliot had managed to get reinforcements to help at the practice.

Her mind drifted to Jeremy. He had done very well in his exams and his average was high. He had a few days before he started his holiday job, but he had got up early to tramp over to the campus library because he had left his genetics book there.

The door to the flat burst open and immediately was slammed. Footsteps were heard running into Jeremy's room and that door crashed shut.

Gabrielle threw back the bedclothes. She was instantly awake. Something odd had happened.

Outside her bedroom in the narrow hallway, the floor was covered in scrip. She bent to pick it up. 'Scrip' was the university's paper money that was exchanged for food. Students bought it at the beginning of term. As it could only be exchanged for food, there was no likelihood that they could use it for other things and then have nothing to eat near the end of term when all their money was low.

Muffled sobs came from her brother's room, and Gabrielle was alarmed. Jeremy was usually so calm; he took everything in his stride. The last time she had seen him cry was at their father's funeral.

Opening the door gently, she saw him lying face down on his pillow.

'Whatever's happened?' She sat on the bed. But he only turned away and hid his face from her.

'Tell me—what is it?' Inside she was panicking. 'All that money in the hall, did you buy it?'

'No—no,' he sobbed loudly.

'Then whose is it?'

'Brooker's. No. . .mine. He's dead.'

Gabrielle had to make some sense of all this, and quickly. She forced her brother to look at her, while she stared into his blotchy swollen eyes.

Between sobs and sharp intakes of breath he told her, 'I went to the fourth floor of Newton. I'd left some books on my carrel, and there he was.'

'Brooker. . .?'

'Yes. He was lying face down on top of the desk. It was a typical position for him. When he was tired he used to. . .' Jeremy broke off again. 'Well, I went up and slapped him on the back to wake him up.' His eyes grew wide with fear. 'Then he just slithered to the floor.'

'He was already dead. But how?'

'Pills. They were on the carrel. He must have

hidden in the library before the weekend and. . .'

'Why on earth did he do it? Brooker was doing so well, with all his high marks.'

Jeremy wiped his face with the back of his hand. 'I found his transcript on his desk. He must have lied. His marks were all low—I mean really low. He barely passed. The only nine he got was for the paper I helped him with.'

Gabrielle felt like crying herself, but she didn't. Mechanically she cradled her brother's head and stroked his hair.

'He left me the scrip,' Jeremy said after a long silence. 'But I don't want it. He put it on my desk in an envelope saying thanks for all my help.' He broke into sobs. 'I didn't help him at all. I never knew.'

'We weren't supposed to know,' Gabrielle said slowly. 'Brooker just kept silent. It must have been the pressure of his parents' expectations.'

Jeremy sat up. 'I don't think I'll be much good as a doctor, Gaby. I should have seen—I should have known.'

She tried to soothe him again. 'How could you possibly know? No one knew. Brooker kept his secret until his death.'

'I'm so shaken up.' Jeremy bit his nails. 'How

shall I ever cope with the dying when I'm treating patients?'

'That'll be quite a different situation,' she said definitely. 'Finding Brooker like that was a terrible shock. Let me make you a hot cup of tea. You're still shaking, and so would I be if I'd found him in those circumstances.'

It took a long time for Jeremy to calm down. With a wretched eye on the clock Gabrielle watched the seconds zoom by. She was due at work that afternoon, but she didn't want to leave Jeremy alone.

'Shall I ring Dr Cougar and say I can't make it into work this afternoon?' she asked.

'No, don't do that!' His voice was shrill. 'It'll be all over campus about the affair and that I found him. I don't want Cougar to think I'm weak or that I can't deal with emergencies. He'd never give me a job then.'

'Oh, Jeremy,' she sighed, 'I'm sure no one will think anything of the sort.'

He started to sob again. 'I can never go back to that part of the Newton again. I could never study there. I'll go to the Medical Library from now on. I won't have a carrel; I'll just sit at one of the big study tables with the others.

Gabrielle understood. 'I'll try and fix something up for you,' she promised. 'If I talk to the

librarian perhaps he'll find you a carrel some-
where else. In the Medical Library, even. . .'

She knew this was a vain hope, but she was
going to try. After soothing her brother some
more, she very reluctantly set off for work.

Brooker's death had shocked her. She felt
she had kept her emotions well in check all
afternoon when she was helping Eliot, but after
the last patient had gone she found an old
magazine in one of the treatment cubicles. On
it she saw a glossy advertisement.

It made her catch her breath, and she had to
sit down shakily. From the brightly coloured
page Brooker posed up at her. She began to
cry.

Eliot's voice interrupted her remembrance.
'Why are you crying?' He spoke gently. 'Have I
upset you?'

She could not speak at first. 'No.'

He sat down beside her, very close. It was
Purgatory to have him near and know he was
about to marry Claudia. And more like hell
with Brooker staring up at her too. She showed
him the picture.

'Brooker was a friend. He committed suicide
in the Newton. Jeremy found him this morning.'

Tears flowed freely. She felt a strong arm
around her shoulders, and she leant into his
body.

'That must have been a shock—for both of you.'

Taking the handkerchief he offered, Gabrielle dried her eyes. 'Neither of us suspected a thing—that was the worst thing. And he'd been very good to me. If it hadn't been for him I don't think I'd have got this job either.'

'What do you mean?' he asked gently.

She explained briefly.

'I didn't know anything about that. I was under the impression you'd been shopping.'

'It doesn't matter now.' Gabrielle blew her nose. 'He was helpful to Jeremy too. If only it hadn't been my brother who found him! Now, on top of everything, he has doubts about his ability to be a doctor.'

Eliot held her closer. The warmth of his body was such a comfort. 'I remember when my first patient died.' He spoke in a whisper. 'I was very upset—I took it personally. But an old doctor explained that death was a part of medicine and that the only way to view it was not to take it personally. I was told to learn from it and to use that knowledge to help other patients. That situation in the hospital is totally different from the one your brother is in.'

'That's exactly what I told him.'

'Yes,' he continued, 'Jeremy will grieve for his friend, then he'll get over it. Student Health run a counselling service for students in trouble—there are advertisements all over campus. More should be done, though. Your Brooker fell through the net.'

Eliot looked at the picture of Brooker modelling summer clothes. 'He looks happy enough here.'

'I don't think he was academically cut out for university,' Gabrielle explained. She told him about Brooker's professor parents.

He looked grave. 'A typical story—children desperately acting out parents' expectations.'

Then he looked directly into Gabrielle's face. His eyes were marvellous. There was something special and compelling about them. It was as if Eliot was filling her with strength. She could feel his strength enter her body.

'I'm sure Jeremy will cope with the sad loss of his friend, and that in time he may even use this experience and become a better and more humane doctor for it. Shall I take you home, Gabrielle?'

She felt more at peace now, thanks to Eliot. She wondered why he was so generous with his time and his emotion. After all, he had Trish to think about too.

It was only a couple of days before Trish's appointment with Professor Straitman. Gabrielle spoke to Eliot about the situation.

'Have you said anything to Trish yet?' she asked.

'Yes. I told her that I'd noticed that her spine wasn't completely straight, and that I thought it a good idea if we went to see someone about it.'

'And what did she say?'

'How right you were, Gabrielle.' He nodded as he spoke. 'She said she knew, and she'd do anything to be straight like everyone else in her class. Apparently there's another girl at the school with scoliosis. She wears a Milwaukee brace.' He grimaced. 'I just hope Trish isn't that far gone.'

The next day Eliot was more tense than Gabrielle had ever seen him. He had managed to speak to Professor Straitman on the telephone.

During the lunch hour it was panic stations. Eliot's patients had been rearranged so that he could attend the consultation with Trish, but another doctor at the practice had suddenly been taken ill, so all *his* patients would attend. And with Claudia away there would be no other doctor to see them.

Eliot, Trish and Gabrielle were all in the reception area when Mrs Pearly took the ill-fated telephone call that said that the other doctor would not be able to attend that afternoon.

'And what am I to do?' rasped Eliot. 'Cut myself in half? I can't be with Trish and here at the practice at the same time!'

Mrs Pearly said quite categorically, 'You need a wife, Dr Cougar. That's what you need.'

Eliot snapped his fingers frantically in the air. 'And where am I to conjure one up from? Tell me that!'

Trish, who had appeared very calm all through her father's ranting, said, 'Don't fret so, Daddy. Gabrielle can take me to see Professor Straitman.'

'This is a family matter. Even if by birth you're my niece, I'm still your father by adoption. And I should be with you.' He tried to keep the anxiety from his voice.

'I know what's going to happen. I've spoken to Claire. She's got scoliosis too.'

Gabrielle knew this must be the girl at Trish's school who wore the brace.

Trish continued, 'I'll have X-rays and photographs today. Nothing much else will happen. And you can have a long talk with Professor Straitman, just as you did the other night.'

After a lot of reasoning Eliot agreed. But he was not altogether reassured that it was the right thing.

Gabrielle quickly changed out of uniform and

into some warm clothes for the short walk across to the university hospital.

As they walked briskly Trish said, 'I'm glad it's you and not Daddy.'

'Why?' Gabrielle was incredulous.

'You've got to keep taking all your clothes off, so you're completely naked. I don't mind in front of you, though.'

Now Gabrielle understood. 'What else has Claire told you?' she asked.

'Oh, everything. Apparently when you have your photograph taken it's awful. You have to bend forward.'

'Don't worry,' Gabrielle assured her. 'I'll be there.'

'I'm going to have loads of X-rays too,' Trish raced on again, sounding a little more cheerful. 'One of my hand to show the age of my bones. That seems odd, but that's how they do it. And to view the spine they take the picture from the back instead of the front so that reduces the amount of radiation to the breasts.'

When they arrived at the clinic Gabrielle explained why she had come and that Eliot was unavoidably detained. The nurse nodded and showed them into the waiting area. It was some time before the professor stepped out of his office and called them in. He was a tall willowy man; Gabrielle guessed that he was about sixty.

His small faded blue eyes were warm and friendly.

'Ah, now, let me see.' He made Trish and Gabrielle sit in front of his desk while he rummaged in the drawers. 'Forgive me if I'm slightly confused. I'm a bit jet-lagged. That hop across the Atlantic. . . Oh, here are my scoliosis forms.'

He asked many questions and noted the answers down. Dates of periods and when the first period had shown were all carefully taken. Trish was shifting nervously in her chair by now. It was taking a long time.

The session in X-ray was tedious. Again they had to wait. Some pile-up on the highway had the radiographers racing around seeing to the emergency patients.

At last the X-rays were finished and duly developed, and the two returned to Professor Straitman. He viewed them with a critical eye and then asked Trish to undress in a cubicle. Gabrielle he kept back.

'Now, my dear, Eliot has told me a great deal. He's an anxious father. I'll need some more answers from you.'

Hurriedly he went on, 'Does Trish like sport?'

Gabrielle thought it lucky that she knew. She told him that she didn't. 'And she hates skiing.

She can't go in a straight line. Is that due to the scoliosis?'

'Undoubtedly. She isn't taking her body weight evenly on both feet.'

'So it's not because she's clumsy or stupid that she can't ski well.'

'No, no, my dear. It's all very logical.'

He examined Trish, then said she must go for photographs. 'She can go to the medical photographer while I examine your back,' he explained to Gabrielle.

'*My* back?' exclaimed Gabrielle.

'Yes, yes. Eliot and I have discussed all this. Didn't he tell you?'

Gabrielle presumed that Eliot had said something about her old back injury, so she began to undress. As Trish was being taken to the photographers she whispered something in the professor's ear. He nodded and sent her on her way.

Gabrielle was concerned for Trish. 'She will have a nurse with her all the time the photographs are taken?' she asked anxiously, remembering the girl's fear.

'Of course, my dear. Really, you and Eliot are just the same—a little over-anxious about Trish. But I can understand. She's a sweet little girl.'

Gabrielle was pleased to hear that there was

nothing wrong with her back. She was about to ask something when a nurse rushed in and said that the professor was needed in the emergency theatre immediately. There was a problem with one of the spinal injuries from the highway crash.

The professor looked a bit harassed. 'Well, my dear, that's that. I must rush. But don't worry—I'll ring Eliot tonight and tell him all about my findings. Go home now. It's been nice meeting you, Mrs Cougar.'

Mrs Cougar. Gabrielle was dumbfounded. Oh, no! He had thought that she was Trish's mother and of course he had looked at her spine to test for scoliosis and the possibility of a hereditary cause.

Before she could put him right he had dashed away and was out of sight.

'What a mix-up!' she told the nurse at Reception.

'Oh, he's a bit addled today.' She laughed. 'And he's new to the hospital. Anyone else would have known that Dr Cougar is a bachelor. I'll tell him when he comes back.'

Gabrielle found Trish, who was all but perky. 'I thought you weren't going to leave me for those photographs,' she complained.

'I'm sorry. But a nurse was with you all the time, wasn't she?'

'Yes.' But Trish looked put out.

It was very late when they arrived back at the practice. Eliot already had his overcoat on.

Gabrielle explained that the professor had been called to an emergency theatre and that he would call Eliot later. She forgot all about the identity mix-up.

Very late that evening when the night was pitch black outside, Gabrielle sat alone in the apartment reading. Jeremy was out celebrating the end of term at a party. She didn't expect him home until the early hours.

He had recovered slightly from Brooker's death, and Gabrielle had told him what Eliot had said. And Eliot's words had been some comfort.

The doorbell sounded imperiously. She thought it was her brother coming home without his keys, so when she saw Eliot she was surprised. But she was even more shocked at the way his eyes glittered. There was something almost wild about him. He looked like a man at the limit of his patience.

CHAPTER NINE

'HAS something happened to Trish?' Gabrielle asked anxiously.

'She's at home with my housekeeper,' came the blunt reply.

There was obviously something terribly upsetting gnawing away inside Eliot. 'Let me take your hat and coat and get you a cup of coffee,' she offered.

As she helped him off with his coat she noticed how taut he was. His muscles were rigid like iron.

'Go into the lounge,' she said. 'I'll put the kettle on.'

He turned sharply and walked away.

In the kitchen she filled the kettle, but all the time she could hear him pacing restlessly up and down.

Gabrielle sat on the chesterfield and tried to make her voice sound soft. She was trying to calm him. 'Please sit here, Eliot. I can see you're desperately worried about Trish.'

He stopped pacing and sat perched on the edge of the chesterfield. 'Of course I'm out of my mind with worry! Straitman told me the curve was twenty degrees. She's already booked into hospital for the Milwaukee brace.' He ran his hand over his chin.

Gabrielle was alarmed. She hadn't guessed that the spine curved that badly. 'Admitting her may seem like a serious step, but I believe it's a Scandinavian idea. They believe it lessens rejection of the brace.'

'The damned brace!' he ground out. She saw his hands tighten into fists on his knees. 'I hate the idea of my little girl in that scaffolding!'

Gabrielle felt very sad too.

He continued, 'A pelvic girdle of steel and leather, another ring around her neck. . .and outriggers of steel running between the two. It's like something from the Middle Ages! And to think she has to wear the thing night and day until she stops growing. . .and even then, if the spine continues to bend she'll have to undergo that major operation to implant a metal rod down her spine.'

She wanted to take him in her arms and soothe him as best she could. But she knew everything he said was true. Nothing she could do could alter those facts.

So she placed her hand lightly over his fist and said softly, 'If there's ever anything I can do, Eliot——'

'Anything?' There was a strange edge to the way he echoed her word.

'Yes, of course.'

'Yes, there's *something*. . .' He spoke as if he was on the edge.

Her eyes searched his for the explanation. Then suddenly she was being kissed, and fiercely. The shock and his roughness took away her breath.

This was Eliot as she had never known him. These kisses were not like the tender ones he had given her on the night of their first kiss, neither were they the sensually thrilling ones that she had received under the sprig of mistletoe. These were fierce and fuelled from frustration.

He broke off and rasped, 'You go around telling people you're my wife, Gabrielle. Well, life is so crushingly serious at the moment that I could do with some physical release!'

His mouth was on hers again, his hand expertly flicking open the buttons on her blouse.

So this was behind his sexual outburst. She tried to push him away. 'It was a mistake——' She was breathless and by now incensed.

Fighting back was useless, however hard she tried. His natural strength and weight far outstripped her own. He was winning, and the increasing heated throb of his high-pitched excitement burned through her clothes.

A thud at the door alerted Gabrielle. 'It's Jeremy. It's my brother!'

It took Eliot a moment to come to his senses. With a jerk he pulled her to a sitting position and hissed, 'Get your clothes on!'

There was no need for that instruction. Already she was fumbling and pulling her blouse into position. Eliot was madly stuffing his shirt back into his trousers.

Jeremy stumbled into the apartment. He'd had a jar too many. 'My God. The place is on fire!' he slurred, and swayed towards the open door of the kitchen. 'It's not smoke—the kettle's boiled dry!'

She heard him clatter past the kitchen table and force a window open.

All too soon he was back in the sitting-room. 'Gaby, are you crazy? Did you fall asleep?' Seeing Eliot, he came to sudden wobbly attention. 'Oh. . . Good evening, Dr Cougar, sir.'

By now Eliot was looking reasonable. At least he had his clothes on, even if his hair was dishevelled. With a calm hand he raked it close to his head. 'Ah, Jeremy, you've been to a party. Did you have a good time?'

Was Eliot mad? thought Gabrielle. Was he

going to embark on pleasant chit-chat? She glared at him.

He ignored her look and carried on. 'Yes, well, we all deserve a little relaxation after a bout of hard work. Good idea, Jeremy.' He said a very quick goodbye and made an equally quick exit.

Jeremy slumped on to the chesterfield next to Gabrielle. 'Sorry—it looks as if the apartment was steaming in two places! Call him back—I don't mind Cougar as an addition to the family.' He was smiling stupidly.

'You don't know what you're talking about,' Gabrielle snapped. 'I'm going to take a shower.'

'Then you're all wrong,' he giggled. 'You undo buttons to take your clothes off. You're doing them up.'

Gabrielle jumped up. 'Shut up, Jeremy!' She stalked off to the bathroom and turned the water on full.

Of all the odious, conceited, arrogant bastards! She now viewed Eliot Cougar from a chilling perspective.

Thank goodness today is the last working day before Christmas, Gabrielle said to herself as she walked into the practice. She didn't know how she would face Eliot after the previous night.

He was talking on the telephone in his office. Immaculate as usual, he sounded very cheerful and relieved as he said, 'Thanks a lot, Professor Straitman. Goodbye.'

Black circles surrounded his eyes. He hadn't slept much last night either.

'About last night. . .' he began apologetically. 'Straitman just put me right about the facts. He can't imagine how he got the idea into his head. But it wasn't you who said you were my wife.'

'Of course not,' Gabrielle bit out. 'I know that, and you could have known it too if you'd only taken the time to listen!'

Eliot stood up and came towards her. She looked him dead in the eye as if challenging him to come further.

He stopped. 'I've felt cruelly ashamed.' His voice was low. 'Can you forget and forgive?'

'I don't think I'll ever forget.' She held his gaze with defiance. 'However. . .' She sighed. 'I can understand that you've been under considerable strain lately.'

He made to come towards her again.

'Don't ever do that again, Eliot!'

She walked out of the office back to Reception. It was hard not to prevent tears spilling down her face. It was ironic. But she wished Claudia had been around. If she had been here,

Eliot would have gone to her. . .and then last night would never have happened.

Working with Eliot had been tense, right up to the time they had wished each other a 'Happy Christmas'. But as Gabrielle left the practice she had no time to dwell on Eliot. She had a purpose in mind, and she marched resolutely right into the Medical Library. She wanted to get Jeremy a new carrel.

When she finally met a librarian who would listen it was like talking to a brick wall. Yes, the woman understood the unfortunate situation. But no. . .Jeremy couldn't have another carrel. There was none available. And no definitely not in the Medical Library. They were like gold dust.

Gabrielle wouldn't give up. She asked for a refund. But this was against library rules.

By the end of the talk the librarian looked jaded. She conceded that Jeremy's case was unusual, and that she would talk to the head librarian. But she didn't know when she'd see him; probably after the holidays.

Gabrielle walked out into the foyer with a head feeling like cotton wool. So she sat on a small row of chairs by the exit.

She was deep in thought when a gentle voice said, 'You here too, Gabrielle?'

She looked up into Eliot's sad kind eyes. He was carrying several large books, all on scoliosis.

'I came to see about a carrel for Jeremy.' She explained the situation. And as she did, she reversed her feelings for Eliot.

Last night he had been a man on the brink. And if only she could have told him the facts about the 'wife' fiasco he would have understood, and definitely not forced her.

'I see you're reading up about Trish,' she remarked.

He compressed his lips and she saw a muscle twitch in his jaw. 'Yes. Professor Straitman called it an ancient and mysterious deformity. The textbooks put it more crudely. They say it was the cancer and the Cinderella of all the orthopaedic conditions.' He shrugged his shoulders. 'Research and the Milwaukee brace have helped a lot recently, though.'

'I'm sure things will turn out fine for Trish.' She tried to sound reassuring.

After they had talked some more they walked past the barriers together.

An alarm bell sounded, and an elderly man in the green and yellow blazer of the university came up. He was a security guard who sat by the exit.

'I think you've forgotten to take your library

books to the desk, Dr Cougar.' He was very
pleasant about it. Obviously Eliot wasn't a
student who was sneaking extra books out.

'Thank you—I did forget,' Eliot apologised.

He excused himself to Gabrielle and returned
to the queue to have the books stamped.

As Gabrielle walked away towards the exit
she looked back over her shoulder. There was
no sign of Eliot. Where had he disappeared to?
He wasn't in the queue waiting to have his
books attended to, and there hadn't been
enough time to have them done already.

It didn't matter. She couldn't be bothered.
He'd probably gone back to look for more
books first. She took a deep breath of the cold
outside air and with an effort struck out for the
apartment.

That evening both she and Jeremy were
quiet. She explained about the carrel.

'Oh, it doesn't bother me,' he said limply. 'I
can study just as well here in the apartment.'

Gabrielle knew this to be untrue. But what
was the point of saying anything?

The telephone rang when she was lounging in
the bath. Moments later Jeremy battered on the
door. 'I've got a carrel! I've got a carrel! And in
the Medical Library!'

Gabrielle pulled a towel around herself and
splashed water all over the floor in her haste.

'Who says? Was that the library? I thought it couldn't be done.'

'It was the supervisor.' Her brother was dancing up and down and around the small bathroom. 'You're wonderful, Gaby! I don't know how you did it—but you did!'

Gabrielle was puzzled. 'I don't know how either.' She supposed it was the unfortunate circumstances. That was her only explanation.

CHAPTER TEN

CHRISTMAS was a quiet affair for Gabrielle and Jeremy. And it had been the same for Eliot and Trish.

Back at work Eliot confided in Gabrielle. 'Today Trish goes into hospital in preparation for her brace,' he told her.

'Wish her luck from me.' Gabrielle sounded as encouraging as she could.

'She's a great little kid,' he added. 'Very philosophical. She says she just wants to be straight like everyone else.' He pushed his hair off his forehead. 'I suppose I have one thing to be thankful for, though.'

'What's that?'

'Straitman examined my back to see if the scoliosis ran through my side of the family.'

Gabrielle dropped her eyelids. Eliot had reminded her of the 'wife' identity fiasco. But his expression bore no remembrance.

'The scoliosis factor must come from my sister-in-law's side of the family. You remember I told you that Trish is my late brother's child?

So I don't think my children will have any problem there.'

'You're thinking of starting a family of your own, then?' She tried to hide her disappointment. Eliot must be about to marry Claudia.

'Yes.' His eyes shone. 'As soon as Trish is settled.'

A week later Gabrielle and Eliot were again talking of Trish. It was the day of her discharge home.

'They've made the Milwaukee brace to your satisfaction, then?' Gabrielle had heard every detail for days.

'Yes. And Trish has been very good—no tears or temper tantrums. Professor Straitman said that it wasn't unusual to have them at the first fitting.'

He was keen to be off to the hospital, so Gabrielle left early too.

Jeremy was recovering well from Brooker's suicide. He still had his quiet moments, but Gabrielle felt relieved that he was not brooding. The Medical Library carrel had helped tremendously.

'It's eleven-thirty.' Gabrielle swilled out the late-night coffee mugs. 'I'm going to bed.'

'I'll just finish some reading.' Jeremy did not

look up as he sat over his books at the kitchen table.

When Gabrielle was in the bathroom she thought she heard the intercom buzz. Jeremy answered and she concluded that it was one of his student friends. She wasn't prepared when he shouted, 'It's Cougar. He's coming up!'

Damn, she thought. And I've taken off all my make-up. She took a moment to drag a brush through her unruly hair. Then she went out to the sitting-room.

Eliot's face was a study in agony. 'It's Trish— I can't do a thing with her. She won't let me take off the brace. She says she won't go to school tomorrow.'

'Brace patients usually have a tantrum at some time,' Gabrielle began.

'She wants you, and only you. Say you'll come. I've got to get the brace off and inspect the skin tonight.' His eyes were wild.

'I'll come straight away,' Gabrielle said definitely.

'Take an overnight bag, in case you have to stay,' Jeremy advised.

'Good idea, Jeremy,' Eliot added.

'Are you sure you'll be all right alone?' Gabrielle asked.

'It seems as if Trish needs you more than I do.'

Gabrielle hurried to her bedroom to pack. She could hear her brother talking to Eliot. 'I don't know much about braces. But at school we had a bloke who had to wear a Lennox-Hill brace for his knee. He hated it at first, couldn't get on with it at all. But after a while he settled into it.'

'Thank you for your concern, Jeremy.' Eliot sounded as if he had recovered some of his composure.

Moments later Gabrielle was being driven at breakneck speed towards Eliot's home.

'Slow down; we don't want to be involved in a crash!' she warned.

Road traffic lights halted their progress, and Eliot drummed irritably on the steering-wheel with his fingertips.

'I don't know what's brought this on,' he said. 'And to think she's got to wear that brace four years full-time and more years part-time. . . If that's a failure she might have to go for that dreadful instrumentation rod that they fix to the spine at operation. I can't bear to think of that.'

'Don't,' Gabrielle said firmly. 'One day at a time—that's the only way to take it.'

Inside the house Eliot was greeted by the old housekeeper, Mrs Bakewell. 'She's still in her bedroom, sir. Sobbing her heart out.'

Eliot bounded up the stairs. Gabrielle found

it hard to keep up. At the bedroom he stopped. 'She's got it locked,' he ground out between clenched teeth.

He was about to pound on the door with his heavy fist when Gabrielle caught his hand. 'The softly, softly approach would be better,' she advised.

'Trish, darling!' he called, making a great effort to remain calm.

'Is Gabrielle there?' It was a little whimpering voice.

'Yes, I'm here.'

After a moment or two when both Eliot and Gabrielle held their breath the door was unlocked.

'Have a drink or something,' Gabrielle advised Eliot.

Reluctantly he obeyed and went downstairs.

When Gabrielle entered the little girl's bedroom she found her standing in the middle of the room. She looked very frightened.

'Get this thing off me, please,' she wailed. 'I feel like a shire horse in harness!'

Gabrielle found the screwdriver and quickly undid all the screws. Patients were screwed in securely and needed the help of another person, which prevented them from taking it off themselves.

'Let's have a look at your skin.' Gabrielle's

nurse's voice came to the fore. She was afraid
of sores.

A red blush, not angry, but quite normal, was
revealed beneath the pelvic girdle. 'That looks
fine.' Gabrielle inspected other areas. 'Everything as it should be.' She handed Trish a
towelling robe. 'Now, why couldn't you let your
daddy do that?'

'I've got my period.' She looked embarrassed.

'I see.' Gabrielle understood. 'Let's run a
bath for you.'

While Trish splashed in the bath Gabrielle sat
close and they talked. After a while Gabrielle
asked, 'Why don't you want to go to school in
the morning?' Refusing to go to school was a
typical rejection reaction against the brace.

'I'll be different. Everyone will pick on me
and bully me. In the hospital there's something
wrong with everyone, so it doesn't matter
there.'

Gabrielle considered this. 'But you've got a
friend there with a brace.'

'Yes, Claire. They tried to bully her. But she
got a boy up against a wall and crushed him so
hard with her body weight and the brace that he
ended up in Casualty with broken ribs.'

Gabrielle had to laugh.

Trish went on, 'I'm smaller than Claire, so I
don't think I can do that.'

They had a long talk, and Gabrielle did her best to bolster the little girl's confidence.

After she had finished her bath Gabrielle put powder on Trish's skin, reapplied the brace and walked with her back to the bedroom.

It took a bit of time to make Trish comfortable. She needed a rolled-up towel beneath her throat-piece and a pillow under her head. Her bed was softer than the one she had been used to in hospital.

Finally, well past one o'clock, Gabrielle found Eliot. She explained the problems. He was particularly worried about the prospect of bullying at school, and so was Gabrielle. Taunts from other children could be even more devastating than a few punches.

He showed Gabrielle into a guest bedroom. 'I wouldn't have been able to cope without you tonight,' he told her.

'There are times when a woman's touch is necessary.'

'Hmm. . .' Eliot leaned against the doorjamb of the bedroom. He looked at his shoes and then at Gabrielle. She thought he would come to her and kiss her, his eyes were so full of desire. 'I'll say goodnight. I'd better look in on Trish.'

Gabrielle was sorry that moment had escaped

them both. Trish and Claudia—they were the two women who took precedence in Eliot's life.

Outside the school gates Eliot wished Trish good luck, and watched as she made her way slowly and awkwardly towards the main entrance.

Gabrielle, sitting in the back seat of the car, watched too. The playground area in front of the school was full of children. All of them turned to look at Trish, and Gabrielle heard Eliot swallow.

From out of the crowd, a tall, very big girl stepped forward and walked towards Trish. This was all that was needed. Trish looked ahead and proceeded resolutely inside the gates. Almost at once a crowd of friends gathered round and they were all talking and laughing in a friendly fashion.

'Wow!' breathed Eliot. 'That was big Claire who came out to see Trish first. I wouldn't dare argue with her. And with a minder like that no one else will bully my daughter!'

Gabrielle was so relieved that she could feel tears moisten her eyes.

'Sit with me in the front, Gabrielle.'

Eagerly she obeyed.

'You've worked a minor miracle with Trish;

could you possibly stay with us for a week or so? We'd both like that so much.'

'I'd love to!' She didn't have to think about it.

'I'll see that you're properly paid, Gabrielle. You can't be expected to do the job for nothing.'

She wouldn't have minded, but money was a problem.

'I'll understand if you want some time off in the evenings to be with your fiancé—Ivan.'

'Ivan?' Gabrielle was startled. 'He's just a friend.'

Eliot looked serious. 'I thought you two were really close. A serious couple.'

'No. I got him back with his old girlfriend. They're getting married soon.'

He was silent for a moment as if taking in the whole situation. 'What's the date today, Gabrielle?'

'January the fourteenth.'

'Right day. Wrong month,' he replied.

She didn't understand. Sometimes he spoke in riddles, especially lately. She presumed he was thinking about his forthcoming wedding to Claudia.

And some evenings later, just as they were leaving work, she was sure she had guessed correctly.

'You take the car home, Gabrielle,' he said. 'I've got plans, and it's important that I see to them immediately. I'll be back early this evening.'

As she drove back to Eliot's place Gabrielle wondered how early. Claudia was due to return to work soon, so no doubt he was spending the time with her.

When she saw Mrs Bakewell she heard that Trish had not come home. The housekeeper was worried. 'It's not like her to be late, miss. Of course, she might have been in and gone out again, perhaps when I was in the basement.'

Although Gabrielle said it was a little too early to get anxious, she certainly felt otherwise.

The last few days in the house had felt perfect to her. It was as if she was a part of the family. Playing Scrabble, helping with homework and late at night sitting with Eliot in front of the log fire had made her very happy. And Jeremy had accepted her absence with delight. She saw him at lunchtimes on campus and so kept up with all his news.

At five-thirty Gabrielle began to ring all Trish's school friends. No, she wasn't with any of them. Mrs Bakewell had a few suggestions, but no luck there either.

It was gone seven when an imperious knock summoned Gabrielle to the front door.

'Oh, Claudia, have you seen Trish?' Gabrielle asked desperately. 'Was she with Eliot?'

'For goodness' sake!' the other woman replied. 'Am I to hear about nothing but that child all the time? No, she wasn't with Eliot when I saw him earlier this evening. Then he wasn't with me for five minutes before he was racing off again.'

'I'm very worried,' Gabrielle told her. 'Trish is usually home by now.'

'You should know,' came the tart reply.

The telephone rang and Gabrielle ran to answer. 'Damn. A wrong number!' She turned, expecting to see Claudia behind. But oddly enough she was stll standing in the hall, preening herself in front of a gold-framed oval mirror. She wore the expression of a sly cat.

'Trish is probably with some doctor friends of Eliot's and mine. I'll call round and see.' She looked smilingly into Gabrielle's eyes and said, 'Be sure to tell Eliot exactly that when he comes home.'

That was a turn-around! thought Gabrielle. Now she's all concerned for Trish.

It was hard sitting and waiting. At eight forty-five Eliot returned. His cool good looks were immediately replaced by a grey concern as he heard the news.

'I'll call the police.' He marched to the phone,

but before he could pick up the receiver it started to ring.

'Claudia. . . What's that you say? Doing what? With Jeremy Ford in the Medical Library? I'm on my way.'

Eliot grabbed Gabrielle by the elbow, then threw her coat to her.

'Where are we going?' she gasped.

'Back to campus. Claudia rang someone and they said they'd seen Trish with your brother.'

'I can't imagine why,' Gabrielle said.

Eliot drove straight up to the Medical Library and yanked Gabrielle out of her seat. 'Jeremy's on the fifth floor,' she called as he ran up the steps ahead of her.

'I know exactly.'

Neither Trish nor Jeremy were near the new carrel.

'There they are—at a big table. Thank God!' Eliot approached calmly.

'Good evening, Jeremy.' Gabrielle knew that tone of cool control. 'Now, Trish, what do you mean by running off and telling no one where you were?'

The girl looked up innocently. 'I left a note on the hall table. Jeremy's been helping me find out things about scoliosis. He's been great. And he took me for supper in the canteen in the Students' Union building.'

'It's way past your bedtime, young lady. And you know you've got a lot to do, what with your exercises and everything,' said her father sternly.

'It's Friday night. You always let me stay up on Fridays.'

'Thank you, Jeremy.' Eliot's voice was a mixture of relief and impatience.

'We were going to phone and let you know where to pick Trish up in a few minutes, sir. Honestly, I wouldn't have let her stay out much later.'

'It seems you at least have some sense,' Eliot said drily.

Downstairs in the car he took up the argument again. 'I didn't like to say too much in front of Jeremy, Trish, but you've had us all frantic! I nearly called the police. I would have if it hadn't been for a neat piece of detective work on Claudia's part.'

'Daddy, I told you—I left a note. It's probably still on the table in the hall.'

'We'll see when we get home. Otherwise you're in hot water,' he said gravely.

Trish didn't seem put out at all. It was as if she knew exactly where the note was. But Gabrielle hadn't seen it.

Trish babbled on as they drove, 'Jeremy showed me how to find the books. You know,

Daddy, there was a really funny old one about scoliosis. A Professor Klapp from Dresden believed people only got the condition because they stood up. Dogs and cats don't get it, you see. So he had all his patients keep on all fours. They even went out in the streets like that. And they had to do types of crawling exercises.'

Eliot's eyes were wide with annoyance. Gabrielle in the back seat could see him in the front mirror. 'Absolute rubbish to treat children like that!' he exploded. 'That man had methods best kept to Noah's Ark and that era. You're fully aware, Trish, that you won't be treated like that nowadays?' Gabrielle winced at his boiling concern.

Laughing, Trish replied, 'Oh, that's exactly what Jeremy said. Modern science is much more advanced. And Jeremy explained about genetic-familial theories behind scoliosis. I wasn't sure if my children would get it. Then we found a picture of a pregnant woman in a modified Milwaukee brace. Did you know, Daddy, if my spine has stopped growing and the scoliosis is stable being pregnant won't harm me?'

Gabrielle saw black eyebrows lower into a black line. 'And what else did Jeremy show you. . .? No, on second thoughts don't tell me! Just be so kind as to inform me of the date of your wedding to Jeremy and the number of children you expect to have.' He sounded thunderous. Gabrielle wouldn't have been in the girl's shoes for the world.

But she only giggled. 'Oh, Daddy, you're priceless! There are two types of men in the world—studs and brothers. Jeremy's like a brother to me.' Remembering Gabrielle in the back seat, she added, 'Sorry, Gabrielle. He *is* like a brother to me.'

'Thank God for that,' growled Eliot. 'Where did you get that choice "studs and brothers" expression from, though?'

'School.'

'I'm beginning to think the boarding-school was better,' he said.

'Oh, no!' Trish wailed. 'I can't go back there. Claire and I are doing a school project on scoliosis—that's why I was at the library. I was getting the information.'

Both Eliot and Gabrielle sighed when the reason for Trish's absence was explained.

At last Eliot laughed. 'Can you keep up with this family and its crazy antics, Gabrielle?'

'Just about,' she replied, and caught the look of fun in his eyes.

Inside the house Mrs Bakewell ran forward to greet everyone. They went all through the explanations again until the old housekeeper came to her usual state of concern about their stomachs and went off to prepare something to eat.

Standing in front of the hall table, Eliot pointed to the notepad and said, 'No note, Trish. You're in trouble.'

Flashing through Gabrielle's mind came the picture of Claudia looking like a sly cat. She took up the nearby pen and made rapid cross-hatching strokes lightly across the top page. Fortunately Trish wrote with a heavy hand and the impression of her writing was revealed. 'Gone to University Medical Library. Will find Jeremy. I'll ring about nine for a lift home.'

Eliot was delighted. 'I'm glad you didn't lie, Trish.' He hugged her. 'I suppose the top page fell on the floor or something.'

Gabrielle blamed herself for not finding the original note. Undoubtedly it had been there all along, until Claudia's entrance. But then she would have known the running of the house better than Gabrielle.

That night Gabrielle lay awake in her bed. She had said nothing to Eliot about the idea that Claudia was to blame for his prolonged anxiety concerning Trish. He still thought the woman doctor was the only person who had led him to find Trish. Gabrielle did not doubt that she had some very vicious ulterior motive for her actions.

The house was quiet. It was very late. She heard Eliot's light footsteps on the landing outside her door. Was it her imagination, or did he stop outside her door? If he did, it was only for a tantalising moment, because seconds later she heard him open and close his own bedroom door softly.

The next morning was Saturday, and for some reason they were to work until twelve at the clinic.

Trish was to spend the day with Claire. They would be working up ideas for their project. Eliot was enormously proud of this idea once he had recovered from the shock of Professor Klapp's exercise routines and the idea of pregnant women in the Milwaukee brace.

He was even happier to find Claudia had put in an unexpected appearance at the clinic. By rights she was not due to return to work until Monday.

Because of her presence they got through the patients in double quick time, and well before lunch Gabrielle was ready to leave. She already had on her overcoat, but at the last minute she found some files that had been left in the wrong place.

It was in the empty Reception that Claudia advanced on her.

'I've underestimated you, Nurse Ford.' Her voice was icy cold and her mouth thin and ugly.

Gabrielle turned to face her adversary.

'I've only been on holiday a couple of weeks and already you've installed yourself in Eliot's house. How clever of you to make yourself indispensable like that to his neurotic child!'

'She's certainly not neurotic,' Gabrielle defended hotly. 'She's like any other little girl with an orthopaedic problem.'

'And you think love and understanding are the answers? Especially if that spills over and includes Eliot?'

Nothing was going to make Gabrielle lose her temper. Claudia was beneath contempt.

'I know it was you who stole the note that Trish left,' she said calmly. 'I know it was you, Claudia. You deliberately tried to get her into trouble and make yourself look good by making Eliot believe you'd found her whereabouts.'

'All's fair in love and war, my dear. You're even more clever than I thought. That's why I've got to get rid of you—you're too much of a distraction.'

Gabrielle was shocked. Whatever was coming next, she was prepared.

'I've made enquiries,' Claudia went on, 'and there's a very good charge nurse position in one of the big hospitals down south. They'll be only

too willing to accept you—I've seen to that.'
She held out the telephone. 'All you have to do
is ring, and the job is yours. It pays substantially
more than your job here.'

Gabrielle was disgusted. 'I'm not leaving—
whatever you try. I'm staying here with my
brother.'

'Ah!' Claudia's voice was a menacing purr.
'Family loyalty—how touching! I'd anticipated
that too. You'll make this phone call—because
if you don't I'll have a word in the Dean of
Medicine's ear.'

Gabrielle started. She knew she wasn't going
to like what she was about to hear.

'Yes.' Claudia's green eyes glowed in antici-
pation. 'The Dean wouldn't like to hear about
your brother's trying to seduce Eliot's daughter
in the Medical Library late at night.'

'That's not true, and you know it! No one will
believe you.' A cold hand gripped Gabrielle's
heart. It might work. A rumour against Jeremy,
even if unsubstantiated, could mean disaster.
Her anger boiled up. She wouldn't allow it. 'I'll
not be subjected to blackmail!' she snapped.
She was so mad that she knocked the telephone
to the floor.

'Foolish. Very foolish.' Claudia picked up the
phone and began to dial.

Gabrielle sprang at her and tore the instrument from her grip. Then they were fighting. Claudia lost her footing and they both slithered to the floor. They had both received slaps one from the other when an angry voice shouted, 'Like two alleycats fighting!' and they were pulled apart and set on their feet.

'Oh, Eliot, darling,' Claudia began, 'she's so jealous! Look—she's scratched my face!' Red livid nail marks bore their trail across Claudia's cheek. And Gabrielle was glad.

Eliot came between the two women, but to Gabrielle's disbelief he turned on her and pushed her towards the front door. 'Get out of here. Go home—take a cab. This will be no place for you. Go!' She was through the door and out into the cold before she could blink.

Her mind was numb. It was as if Eliot had punched her on the head. Without looking back she hurried to the cab rank in front of the university hospital. There were always yellow cabs waiting there. As if in a dream she followed his instructions and soon arrived at his house.

Once inside the front door she was so angry that she determined to pack her suitcase and leave. As her foot trod on the first step of the staircase she stood still. If she left, then Claudia would win. No—she would stay. Eliot would return soon and she would tell him the truth.

Determinedly she marched up the stairs and changed into trousers and a shirt.

Her resolve was short-lived. His words echoed in her head. 'This will be no place for you.' He had certainly spelled out his meaning. Thoughts welled up in her mind, so much so that she found it impossible to think straight.

I need something to eat. I need energy for the confrontation with Eliot, she thought, and went downstairs to the kitchen.

The house was empty. Trish was with Claire, Mrs Bakewell was with her sister and Eliot was. . . Gabrielle couldn't bear to think what he was doing.

In the fridge she found ham. It made a delicious-looking sandwich, but she hardly tasted it as she mechanically chewed and swallowed.

Mrs Bakewell had stored the ham in the fridge on its oven-to-table bakeware. The dish was full of cooking fat stuck to its sides. Gabrielle longed for something to do. This interminable waiting for Eliot was driving her crazy. She would wash the bakeware. It would need a lot of scouring. That would work off some of her over-active thoughts. She had to be calm when he arrived.

She knew Mrs Bakewell kept rubber gloves in the cupboard under the sink. Yes, there were several pairs hanging on hooks. She picked up the nearest pair to hand and put the right one on. It was several sizes too big and her little finger came up against something hard. It was a cent or an old-fashioned British sixpence. She extricated it, and when at last she saw the object she gasped.

'No. . .oh, no!' She felt weak and had to sit at the kitchen table. The object stared up at her. It was a gold skull-and-crossbones ring.

So Eliot was her highway doctor. The very one who had saved her life at the time of the car explosion. Her eyes filled with tears.

She had lost out doubly. She had loved her skull-and-crossbones doctor and she had loved Dr Eliot Cougar. They were one and the same person, and now he was lost to Claudia.

How blind could I have been? she sobbed to herself. Memories became vivid. Her highway doctor had said he had a daughter with a macabre sense of humour. . .that was Trish. He had made the stretcher for Gabrielle from bookshelves. . .they were the ones in Trish's bedroom that had a spooky story to them, a story she had never heard.

By now Gabrielle's head ached. She felt devastated. Slowly she placed the gold ring in the breast pocket of her shirt, then made her way upstairs to wash her face.

No sooner had she done so than she heard the front door bang. 'Gabrielle! Gabrielle!' She heard Eliot shouting and running from room to room looking for her.

He was pounding up the stairs when she came to her door. She dreaded meeting him. Her heart beat frantically.

'Here you are. Why didn't you answer me?' Without waiting for a reply he pushed her on to her bed and sat beside her.

Coldly and with much effort she looked him in the eyes. 'When do you want me to leave the practice?' she asked.

'It's Claudia that's leaving, not you. She's got a job in research in the East. She'll be working on artificial intelligence. . .robots. That'll suit her. You're staying with me.' He was out of breath and panting, but his voice was masterful.

'I don't understand,' Gabrielle began. 'I thought she was your fiancée.'

'Never! Claudia's weapons of love are too sharp for me. I heard everything over the intercom. I'd just switched it on when that little scenario followed.'

'But you told me to leave, that I wasn't welcome.'

He touched her cheek gently. 'The air was blue when I got through with Claudia. It certainly wasn't a place for you, my love.'

He had called her his love, and she was deliriously happy.

'Now listen, Gabrielle. I was going to propose to you on February the fourteenth—Valentine's Day. But that's too far in the future. I've got some things on order, a diamond and a wedding ring, but they're not ready yet. I've asked Jeremy if he'll be best man, and he will——'

'Stop!' she said laughingly. 'Have you asked me?'

'I'm asking you now.' His eyes were serious.

'Of course.' She kissed him in such a way as to leave him in no doubts. He was hungry for her kisses, but she pulled away and felt in her breast pocket. 'I have a ring for you,' she told him.

'Is it Leap Year?' he asked curiously. Then he saw the ring. 'Where did you find it? Trish gave it to me, but I lost it.'

She told him. 'And I fell in love with you, Eliot, when you wore it at my accident.'

He looked incredulous. 'You mean you were my patient that day, Gabrielle? But you looked different.'

'I've had my hair cut since, and I was covered in flour.'

'Yes.' He laughed softly, then brushed her curls away from her temple. 'Yes, there is a very slight scar here. I looked for you. I rang the hospital. . .'

'I wanted to go back to the one where I'd worked,' she explained.

He slipped the skull-and-crossbones ring on his finger. 'I might have known! When we kissed under the mistletoe at Christmas I felt a very strong feeling then. . . But I never guessed. How strange life is!'

Gabrielle thought of Trish. 'How will Trish react to me as a mother?'

'Oh,' he slippd his arms around her waist, 'she's overjoyed. It seems she played a trick on you at Professor Straitman's clinic. She told him you were her mother. Don't be too cross with her. . .although I think I nearly lost you when I behaved like a bastard to you that night.'

'Don't think about that,' she said softly.

'One more thing, Gabrielle. . . I think we must have a dinner party soon. The Dean of Medicine will want to meet my future brother-in-law. Jeremy will have no problem with his interview for med school after that.'

'It was you!' Gabrielle's eyes filled with loving. 'You got Jeremy the carrel in the Medical Library.'

'Yes. I couldn't have anyone close to you upset.'

'I love you so much, Eliot.' Their kisses were deep and long.

'Studs and brothers,' Eliot said huskily. 'I don't feel at all like a brother to you, Gabrielle.'

'Good,' she whispered. 'I don't feel like a sister either.'

A wicked glint flashed in his eyes as he carried her into his bedroom.

Underneath the bedcovers he turned her on her side. 'Young ladies with bad backs should have considerate lovers.'

'My back doesn't hurt.'

'Good. And I'll see it never does. A painful back can make lovemaking a misery.'

She wasn't afraid of the strength and the power of Eliot's body. He was an exciting yet considerate lover. And when she gave her innocence to him it was only a short sharp pain which she accepted because she wanted all of him.

They made love and slept in each other's arms, and in the early morning light when his eyes said, Let's make love again, she stroked the thick black hair on Eliot's chest and moved her hands lower. 'Now you really are my skull-and-crossbones lover.'

Three women, three loves . . . Haunted by one dark, forbidden secret.

ALIX ATKINSON

Boundaries

Margaret – a corner of her heart would always remain Karl's, but now she had to reveal the secrets of their passion which still had the power to haunt and disturb.

Miriam – the child of that forbidden love, hurt by her mother's little love for her, had been seduced by Israel's magic and the love of a special man.

Hannah – blonde and delicate, was the child of that love and in her blue eyes, Margaret could again see Karl.

It was for the girl's sake that the truth had to be told, for only by confessing the secrets of the past could Margaret give Hannah hope for the future.

W🌐RLDWIDE

4 MEDICAL ROMANCES
AND 2 FREE GIFTS
From Mills & Boon

Capture all the excitement, intrigue and emotion of the busy medical world by accepting four FREE Medical Romances, plus a FREE cuddly teddy and special mystery gift. Then if you choose, go on to enjoy 4 more exciting Medical Romances every month! Send the coupon below at once to:

> **MILLS & BOON READER SERVICE, FREEPOST**
> **PO BOX 236, CROYDON, SURREY CR9 9EL.**
> No stamp required

✂- ✂

YES! Please rush me my 4 Free Medical Romances and 2 Free Gifts! Please also reserve me a Reader Service Subscription. If I decide to subscribe, I can look forward to receiving 4 Medical Romances every month for just £5.80 delivered direct to my door. Post and packing is free, and there's a free Mills & Boon Newsletter. If I choose not to subscribe I shall write to you within 10 days – I can keep the books and gifts whatever I decide. I can cancel or suspend my subscription at any time. I am over 18.

EP02D

Name (Mr/Mrs/Ms) _____

Address _____

_____

_____ Postcode _____

Signature _____

MILLS & BOON